KT-443-856

GAMBLER FOR HIRE

When the cards are not running his way, Dan Largo puts himself up for hire. But when Elinora Langford asks him to take her to Skull Pass, he refuses. The land is sacred to the Apache and noone comes out alive. However, when a game of blackjack turns bad-tempered and Largo faces a lynch rope, Elinora saves his neck. Beholden to her, Dan escorts her to Skull Pass. But all the warnings of the dangers come true, and Dan soon wonders if death isn't too high a price to pay for promised treasures.

RIO BLANE

GAMBLER FOR HIRE

WARWICKSHIRE
COUNTY LIBRARY

CONTROL No.

Complete and Unabridged

LINFORD
Leicester

First published in Great Britain in 2001 by
Robert Hale Limited
London

First Linford Edition
published 2003
by arrangement with
Robert Hale Limited
London

The moral right of the author has been asserted

Copyright © 2001 by James O'Brien
All rights reserved

British Library CIP Data

Blane, Rio
   Gambler for hire.—Large print ed.—
Linford western library
1. Western stories
2. Large type books
I. Title
823.9'2 [F]

ISBN 0–7089–9436–9

Published by
F. A. Thorpe (Publishing)
Anstey, Leicestershire

Set by Words & Graphics Ltd.
Anstey, Leicestershire
Printed and bound in Great Britain by
T. J. International Ltd., Padstow, Cornwall

This book is printed on acid-free paper

This one especially for Tina

1

'Seems to me, mister,' the man sitting across the blackjack table from Dan Largo said, his grey eyes getting meaner by the second, 'that your luck's held a mite too long.'

Rupe Lambert's gaze settled sourly on the king and ace that Largo had turned up to beat his pair of tens. His glare challenged the other gamblers at the table.

'You figure so, gents?'

A triple-chinned man who had lost heavily due to wild betting grumbled, 'Now that you say so, Rupe . . . '

Two other men studied the baize table. Lambert threw down the gauntlet to them.

'You fellas gone dumb?'

The other gambler at the table, a tall distinguished man with a beard trimmed to perfection said, 'You shouldn't play cards if you can't appreciate a man's luck, Rupe.'

'Come to think of it, you ain't lost as much as the rest of us, have you Doc?' Lambert griped.

This got the table-gazers' attention.

One of them, Larry Keane, a farmer who hadn't the poke to be in a game of blackjack to begin with, growled, 'Rupe's right, Doc.'

'I haven't been as wild as you gents,' Lonergan reasoned.

The farmer's eyes shifted between Largo and the man with the beard. Then he dismissed his thoughts.

'Naw. The doc ain't in league with this stranger, Rupe. Docs don't cheat.'

Lonergan laughed, a deep rumbling laugh that was evidence of the man's easy-humoured nature.

'Well, now, Larry. I've known a few who'd cheat the devil and sell their mother into slavery.'

'Yeah?' Keane asked, wide-eyed. 'You're kiddin', Doc. Ain't yah?'

'He ain't kiddin',' the second table-gazer growled. 'I knowed a doc once who was the crookedest card-handler I ever knowed,' he griped. 'That bastard had more aces up his sleeve than a rattler's got spits.'

Dan Largo waited, making no attempt to claw in the pot he'd just won. Reaching for it could cause all sorts of mayhem. But he wasn't giving up on it; he was just letting the other gamblers blow steam. Sometimes a little steam-blowing was all that was needed to settle a man down. Other times . . .

He caught sight of Elinora Langford entering the hotel lobby through the open door of the gambling room and, not for the first time, he pondered her fine figure. Elinora Langford was the kind of woman a man could spend a long winter with and never feel the cold.

She nodded in his direction, and he returned her greeting.

'Are you for hire, Mr Largo?'

Elinora Langford's earlier question came back to him.

'Depends on what you need doing,

ma'am,' he'd replied, keeping a tight rein on the direction his mind was taking, before he realized that Elinora Langford would have no need of making the kind of proposition to a man that preoccupied his thoughts. He recalled now with a wry smile her musical laughter.

'You're a fine man, true enough, Mr Largo. However, I've got more trouble kicking men out of my bed than I do hauling them in.'

Largo did not doubt the veracity of her boast for a second.

'And drop the ma'am, sir. My name,' Dan Largo's hand still felt the warm caress of her handshake, 'is Elinora Langford.'

'Miss?' he had enquired, instantly.

'Mrs,' she had replied with equal alacrity.

Largo recalled how his spirits had plummeted. And how they had been boosted over the moon a second later when she clarified.

'Widowed.'

'Sorry,' he'd said.

'No, you're not,' she'd replied.

'No, I'm not,' he'd admitted.

'Now that that's out of the way,' Elinora Langford said, 'about this proposition, sir.'

'That'll be Dan . . . Elinora.'

'OK, Dan,' she agreed after a moment's consideration. 'Are you for hire?'

'No.'

'The sheriff told me that you hire out for tasks, once the pay's right.'

'Sheriff Baldwin is right. But, you see, right now I'm waiting for a game of blackjack to begin. I figure that when I have a choice, playing cards is safer than being shot at.'

'Who said anything about being shot at?'

Dan Largo had laughed.

'I guess there's a first time for everything. It's been my experience, Elinora, that when a body needs to hire a fast gun it means only one thing. There's an even faster gun around the next corner.'

His laughter had deepened.

'Maybe even two or three.'

'Have you heard of Skull Pass?'

'Can't say I have,' he'd replied.

'You know the territory?'

'Pretty much.'

After a moment's hesitation she had produced a parchment of a roughly-drawn map for his perusal. An X marked the place called Skull Pass.

'It's what my Uncle Willie called the place. Know it?'

'Uh-huh. It's got different names to different folks, and no name at all to some. It's sacred ground to the Apache. I guess Uncle Willie's name for it fits the bill nicely.'

Elinora Langford had said, 'I want you to take me there.'

Dan Largo had looked carefully at her. She didn't look *loco*. But she had to be if she wanted to go to Skull Pass. Anyone who wanted to go there was only fit for locking up, for their own good.

'One thousand dollars,' she'd said.

'Another thousand when we reach the pass. How long will it take?'

Her mood was confident, assuming that the lure of one thousand dollars to a gambler would prove too much to resist. To most it would have.

'Doesn't matter,' Largo had drawled. 'I'm not going anywhere near Skull Pass, Elinora. You'd need rocks inside your head to go there.'

He had stepped back a pace. 'You don't look crazy.'

'Aren't you interested why I'd want to go there?' she'd enquired, taken aback by Largo's casual dismissal of a thousand dollars.

'No,' he'd answered. 'I learned a long time ago that in this country a man should only know what he needs to know, if he wants to live a long life.'

'Dan,' she'd purred, and he felt his resolve melt like spring snow, 'two thousand dollars, now. Two thousand when — '

He had held up his hands to stop her, before temptation became too acute to resist.

' 'The problem is, Elinora, that money isn't any use to a dead man. Few men have made it to Skull Pass and lived. Fewer still have ridden into the pass and survived. Like I said, Uncle Willie named it well.'

'You in or not, mister?' Rupe Lambert had called out, as Largo had dallied with Elinora Langford.

'I'm in,' he'd called back.

'Then let's play cards,' Lambert had growled, and to much amusement. 'I reckon you're going to need all the shekels you can get your hands on to court that fine filly you're gabbing with.'

Largo had tipped his hat.

'Nice chatting, Elinora.'

'Three thousand dollars!'

Dan Largo had paused mid-stride. Well, mention of three thousand dollars did that to a man. He'd turned slowly, much tempted. Then, fortunately for him, came the bad news.

'Of course, I'll need to realize the assets I expect my venture to bring in to pay you in full.'

'Ah!'

'I never welsh on a deal.'

Elinora Langford jutted her hips in an age old message that sent a tremble through Dan Largo. Confident that she'd ensnared him with the promise of other benefits added to monetary gain, she smiled, smugly.

Largo liked women the same as every other red-blooded male, and more than most. However, he did not like cocky women, and Elinora Langford was one cocky woman. She strolled towards him, hips swaying, eyes smouldering, breasts heaving. She took a stance in front of him, legs apart.

'You in?' she purred.

Largo's eyes ran over every inch of her body, coming to rest at the apex of her separated legs.

'I'd sure like to be,' he'd crooned.

Elinora Langford smirked, her cockiness notching up a good ten points.

'Come to my room in fifteen minutes.'

Her purr had been pure alley-cat.

9

'Elinora honey,' Largo had smiled, 'when you go fishing you use every bit of bait you've got, don't you?' He sighed. 'Thing is, a fish only bites when it's hungry, and I'm not hungry, Elinora.'

He turned to enter the gambling room.

'Where're you going?' she had asked, at first amazed. Then anger glowed on her cheeks. She wasn't a woman used to rejection, and took it badly.

'To play blackjack,' he'd replied, not at all sure if the excitement of turning good cards could outweigh the pleasures that Elinora Langford promised.

'You got an explanation, mister?'

Rupe Lambert's snarled question brought Dan Largo's attention back to the trouble on hand.

'My deal's clean,' he told him.

'What if I say it ain't?' Lambert growled.

Then tension around the table notched up. The other gamblers, except Doc Lonergan, eased back their chairs from the table. Other games in the room had died. Lambert's challenge had earned the attention of those in the hotel lobby too, and a knot of onlookers had gathered at the edges of the door, careful to remain out of the line of fire from the expected gunplay.

Elinora Langford smiled wryly at Dan Largo. She was enjoying his predicament.

'Is that what you're saying?' Largo asked in a quiet voice.

Rupe Lambert licked parched lips. There had been a change in Largo that was barely noticeable. He began to sweat. He was feeling suddenly trapped. He knew he had overreached himself, but pride would not let him back out.

'I got chores!'

Larry Keane, the farmer, pushed back his chair and scampered from the room.

'Me, too.'

Another man followed on Keane's coat-tails.

Intrigued, Doc Lonergan remained

seated. Largo would be fast, as a gambler had to be. He wondered if Largo knew whom he was up against? Probably not. The medico figured that it wouldn't matter if he did know. The gambler had the quiet resolve of a man who did not seek out trouble, but if it came a-calling, he'd not back away from it.

Rupe Lambert was the only son and only offspring of Charles Lambert, the territory's richest man. Charles Lambert had built an empire from a one-steer beginning, and had fought off opponents with equal ferocity to build his empire. His business interests were now varied and far-flung, and his bank account was fat enough to fix any wrong that his weak-willed son perpetrated. And if money didn't buy Rupe Lambert out of trouble, his father had no qualms about solving the problem by other means. In Rupe Lambert's past lay a couple of killings that rightly bore the tag of murder, but witnesses had changed their stories and moved to greener pastures as a result, and those who had not were buried beneath those green pastures.

Once, Charles Lambert had been in Lonergan's infirmary, the victim of a bushwhacker acting as an agent for another rancher who was in the throes of a range war with Lambert. He had suffered a wound from which he had been lucky to survive, and luckier still to have had Horatio Lonergan's surgical skills at his disposal. During this time they had formed a friendship, in as much as a man of Charles Lambert's dogmatic persuasion could form a friendship with any man, and he had spoken to Lonergan about Rupe's pampering, and his fears for his son.

'Rupe ain't able to look after himself, Doc,' he'd sighed. 'I wish he was stronger, but he ain't.' He had then confided. 'I worry about when I'm gone. When I'm not around to clean up his messes.'

At a critical moment in his recovery, he had gripped Lonergan by the hand.

'Look out for Rupe when you can, Horatio,' he had pleaded.

Lonergan had extolled the virtues of letting Rupe Lambert account for his own wrongdoing, but finding no joy, had promised to help if he could.

Rupe Lambert did not amount to much, but he'd amount to a lot less in a pine box. And the man who put him there, Lonergan reckoned, would be taking harp lessons soon after.

Lonergan had heard of Dan Largo. He wasn't a gun for hire in the strict sense of the word, but on occasion, when shekels were in short supply he had been known to take on tasks in return for *dinero*: tasks that had usually ended in gunplay — gunplay never initiated by Largo, but always ended by him.

Talk was, on a stroll he'd taken to the hotel porch for a breath of fresh air a while back, that the very beautiful Elinora Langford had made Largo an offer of several thousand dollars to act as her escort and protector on a journey deep into Apache territory, which he'd refused. Sensible fella, Lonergan figured. Why anyone would want to knock on hell's door beat him. But he reckoned that a woman like Elinora Langford would go right into hell itself if need be, and slap the devil's face to get what she had set her mind on getting.

If he was younger, he'd have gone. Because the friendship and favour of a woman like Elinora Langford would, he reckoned, be worth a man risking his hide for the privilege of acquiring.

'Yeah. I guess I'm calling you a low down skunk of a cheat,' Rupe Lambert said, in reply to Largo's question of a moment before.

Lonergan's attention shot back to the present. Rupe Lambert was a grown man of twenty-five, with the marbles of a baby. He hated seeing a man die simply because he was too numb-skulled to back out of a no-win situation, and that's what going up against Dan Largo was.

Rupe Lambert was gun-handy enough, but not in Largo's league, Lonergan reckoned. He'd lay money on the gambler being rattler-spit quick. He was certain that Rupe Lambert would be dead before his hand touched iron.

Lonergan would have preferred to have been called on to honour his promise to Charles Lambert in less danger-laden circumstances, like a town bust-up, of which there had been many. Ruckuses that had not needed his intervention as urgently as the present confrontation did. Rupe Lambert had the kind of nature that was always bucking for trouble. But there was trouble . . . and then there was *trouble*.

'I'm sure Rupe didn't mean to call you a cheat, Mr Largo,' the medico said. 'He's just got a little hot under the collar, the way a man gets if the cards aren't running for him. Isn't that so, Rupe?'

'I can understand that, Doc,' Largo said sociably, accepting the medico's role of peacemaker, and hoping that Lambert would take the opening on offer to withdraw. 'I'm not above the odd cantankerous moment myself.'

His gaze went to Rupe Lambert for confirmation of what Lonergan had just said. It wasn't there. In fact, his eyes held the glint of insanity that a man gets when his reason and good sense desert him, and pride prods him into foolishness, even though that foolishness would surely kill him.

'Rupe,' Lonergan said, with little hope of being heeded. 'Don't do anything silly now.'

'I'm saying he's a card-fixing bastard, Doc,' Lambert growled.

Largo sighed heavily.

'I was hoping you wouldn't say that, mister.'

Lambert stiffened his challenge to the gambler.

'Well, I've said it. You admitting to it?'

'No,' Largo said. 'It isn't true. I deal a clean game. Always have.'

Doc Lonergan's hand slid inside his coat, and though the movement was as slick as snake oil, Dan Largo did not miss it. The gambler figured on the medico packing one of those fancy ladies' guns in his waistcoat pocket. He wondered what side Lonergan was about to come down on? He had played a peacemaker's role up to now. However, the medico had taken a keen interest in his challenger's welfare, as if he'd been obliged to do so. So, until the fog cleared and sides were taken, he'd have to reckon on two guns against him.

'Your move, mister,' Largo told Rupe Lambert. He stood up and swept back his coat to reveal a low slung Colt Peacemaker. 'You make it when you want. Just keep in mind that there's still time to back off. No hard feelings.'

'I'm not going anywhere,' Rupe Lambert spat.

'If that's the way of it,' Dan Largo intoned calmly. 'Go for iron!'

'I'm not going to play second-fiddle,

mister,' Rupe Lambert snarled. 'You call it.'

'If I do that. You won't stand a chance,' Largo chillingly predicted.

The gambler's ice-blue stare sent a shiver through Rupe Lambert that rumbled hollowly in his gut. With his crow-black hair and sharpish, pale features, he looked like death's messenger.

The atmosphere in the gambling room crackled with tension. Gunfights in Spicer's Crossing, though fewer of late with the coming of sterner law and order in the form of US marshals and circuit judges, had not been unusual. It was a border town, and had been a haunt for many hardcases on their way across the Rio Grande. However, this was a gunfight with a difference. The man who had thrown out the challenge was none other than Charles Lambert's son. Most gunfights had been between fellas whose names were unknown and no one cared. They went into unmarked graves to be forgotten about. But if

Rupe Lambert caught lead fatally, the man who planted him might as well turn his gun on his own head. It would be preferable to waiting for Charles Lambert to come after him.

'Count to three, Doc!' Lambert ordered.

'Now, Rupe?' Lonergan placated.

'Start the counting, you old bastard!' Lambert screamed. 'Or so help me, you'll be the first dead man.'

A Derringer flashed in Lonergan's mitt. Lambert scowled darkly.

'You leave me no choice, Rupe,' the medico said.

'Put that damn toy away, Doc!' Lambert scoffed. 'I can take this tin-horn gambler.'

'No, you can't,' Largo warned.

'He's right,' Lonergan said. 'And I'm not going to let you throw your life away, Rupe.'

Without further ado Lonergan grazed Lambert on the thigh with the Derringer. He hobbled about, howling and cursing.

'Don't take on so,' Doc said. 'It's only a flesh nick. I'll have you as good as new before you know it.' He stood up and offered his support to Lambert. 'Come along to my office.'

'I'll get even with you for this, Doc,' Lambert growled.

'No, you won't,' Lonergan predicted. 'Once that fool pride of yours goes off the boil, you'll thank me that you're still sucking air.'

He addressed Largo. 'You will too, mister.'

'I already am. I'm obliged to you, Doc.'

Lonergan enquired of the gambler.

'You ever heard of Charles Lambert?'

'I've heard,' Largo confirmed.

'Well then you know that if you'd sunk lead in his only boy and heir you couldn't run far enough to hide.'

Not knowing who his challenger had been, Dan Largo had to admit to the truth of what the doc had said. There had been a whole host of fellas killed by Charles Lambert for a lot less than

21

planting his son.

'I can handle my own trouble!' Rupe Lambert snarled.

The sheriff arrived in a frenzy of hustle and bustle. Ed Baldwin had timed his entrance to perfection. Over the years he had perfected a routine that had him arriving just at the tail-end of trouble. He had spent twenty years working towards his pension and, with six months to go to his retirement, he wasn't going to step between any gun-toters now. He was looking forward to sitting in that fine rocker he'd made for himself. He'd do, or not do, whatever it took to get his butt safely on it.

Right now that meant taking Rupe Lambert's side.

'You ain't welcome in this town no more, Largo,' he growled, ignoring Doc Lonergan's telling of events in which he placed the blame firmly on Lambert for the ruckus. 'The gambler do that?' Baldwin asked, pointing to the show of blood on Lambert's thigh.

'No, I did,' Lonergan-said, stonily, his low opinion of the sheriff showing on his face.

'That was a damn fool thing to do, Doc,' Ed Baldwin opined. 'Mr Lambert won't like it none.'

'I guess he won't,' Lonergan agreed. 'But it was that or a pine box for Rupe. I reckon when it's explained to his pa, he'll agree that a nicked thigh is a whole lot better than filling a hole in the ground.'

Baldwin scratched at his week-old stubble.

'You know, Doc. I figure you should spend time in a cell 'til Charles Lambert makes up his mind about what you did. Otherwise my butt could be in a sling.'

He shifted uneasily under the medico's fiery gaze.

'You gotta understand my position, Doc. Mr Lambert will want to know what I did when he hears his boy got shot.'

Horatio Lonergan's fiery gaze turned

to one of utter contempt for the whining marshal.

'You know, Baldwin,' he growled. 'By the time you retire there's going to be a mountain of shit in this town, the way you keeping dirtying your pants!'

Another man, the butt of raucous laughter and jibing, would have had his pride prodded enough to lash out at his insulter, but not Ed Baldwin. He had been back-tracking for so long it was second nature to him.

He laughed along with the crowd.

'Get out of my way!' Lonergan pushed the lawman aside. 'I've got a patient to attend to.'

Rupe Lambert got his say in.

'You're right, Baldwin, you old maggot! My daddy is going to be looking for a whole lot of answers.'

Caught between fear and self-protection, Ed Baldwin reacted badly. He drew iron on the doc's back.

'You're goin' to jail Doc. Until Mr Lambert's got his say.'

'No, he isn't.' Dan Largo had spoken

in a whisper, but his voice carried above the baying crowd. His hand hovered over his Peacemaker. 'The doc did nothing wrong. A man doesn't go to jail for saving a man's life, Sheriff.'

The room was filled with fire-cracker tension.

'I've got a drawn gun,' the lawman quipped. 'You figure you can beat a drawn pistol?'

'When it's shaking like the one you're pointing, yes,' Dan Largo answered coolly. He notched up the tension. 'Are you confident that you can squeeze that trigger before I clear leather, Sheriff?'

'I figure I can,' Baldwin stated in a strong voice, but his eyes held doubt.

'Don't add foolishness to foolishness, Baldwin,' Horatio Lonergan counselled. 'I'll patch Rupe up, he'll ride on home, and that'll be an end of it.'

'Don't you listen, Sheriff,' Rupe Lambert goaded the lawman. 'I'll come looking, if my daddy don't.'

Baldwin tried to swallow, but his mouth was dry. He knew the veracity of

Rupe Lambert's statement. If his old man chose to ignore the happening, he would not. Rupe Lambert was a spiteful cur who bore a grudge for a long time, and the longer it festered the meaner he became. He'd killed men for the way they'd looked at him. Only the night before he had had a man held down while he beat him senseless. The man's only crime was that he had brushed against Lambert and spilled his beer.

The thing was, if he went up against Dan Largo, he'd become a daisy-pusher, pronto. And if he did not face up to Largo, well, he'd become a daisy-pusher anyway, only a little later. When Rupe Lambert or his father took their revenge.

He was in one hell of a bind.

Rupe Lambert taunted the sheriff. 'You're hand gone crippled?' He snorted. 'You're right, Doc. The town is going to be full of shit before our shaking sheriff retires.' His eyes narrowed and bored into the lawman. 'That might be sooner than you think, Baldwin. And I figure it'll be a permanent retirement, too.'

Ed Baldwin blanched. He looked deep into Dan Largo's eyes and saw death. Gun in hand or not, he was not going to be standing a second from now if he followed through on his threat to the gambler. As always, he settled for second best, and hoped Rupe Lambert would approve.

'Get out of town right now!' he ordered Largo.

'It's getting late in the day to be hitting the trail, Sheriff,' Largo said. 'I'll leave tomorrow.'

'I said now!'

'And I said tomorrow, Sheriff.'

The gambler scooped up the black-jack pot in his hat. He strolled to the cashier to cash in his chips, leaving Baldwin tussling with a quandary. Eyes switched between the gambler and Baldwin. Largo had offered his back to the sheriff, and those who knew Baldwin well, knew that that was a big mistake.

Dan Largo felt the familiar shiver between his shoulders that had so often kept him breathing. He spun in a low crouch, his Peacemaker leaving leather faster than the eye could see, just as Ed Baldwin's bullet whined overhead and shattered the gilt mirror behind the cashier's booth. A sharp intake of breath rose from the watchers. Largo had the lawman cold in his gun-sights. Baldwin knew that the gambler could kill him with no questions asked. In the West, shooting a man in the back earned total revulsion for the perpetrator of what was considered to be a heinous and cowardly act. Sympathy nor succour would be Baldwin's lot. Dan Largo could pull the trigger and walk away a free man. The sheriff flung his gun aside in the hope of placating the gambler.

Largo fumed at Baldwin's dirty tricks and had to work flat-out to quell the temptation to kill him. But he wasn't a man worth killing. Instead, he walked to where the shaking sheriff stood and laid the barrel of his gun across his right cheek. Baldwin crumpled to the floor nursing his gashed cheek. No one went to help him.

Before Lonergan left with Lambert, the latter promised, 'This ain't over 'tween us, Largo.'

'It is for me,' the gambler replied stonily. 'If you have any sense it will be for you too.'

The bustle dying down, Elinora Langford approached Largo.

'Seems to me that blackjack isn't the easy money you thought it was going to be, Dan.'

He turned from the cashier's window and flicked the thick wad of dollar bills he had got in exchange for his chips. He smiled.

'Easier than riding into hell, Elinora honey.'

'Now that you'll be leaving town . . . you will be leaving town, won't you?'

He considered the wad of bills.

'Guess there's nothing left to keep

me around. Looks like I've cleaned out a lot of pockets.'

'You'll be for hire, then?'

'Not for what you've got in mind, Elinora.'

'Are you saying that you're afraid to ride to Skull Pass?'

'You bet,' he said.

'I don't believe that.'

'You'd better, Elinora. Riling Apaches isn't a sensible or wise thing to do.'

'Apaches don't scare me!'

He believed her. He had formed the opinion that Elinora Langford wasn't an easily scared woman.

'They should. Scare you witless at that.'

Elinora Langford changed tracks.

'OK. I guess I'll have to accept that you're not going to help me. So how about me buying you a drink?'

'I normally buy my own, but . . . '

'Say in ten minutes?' Elinora purred, and it was a purr that started a fire in Largo. 'In my room?'

It was probably the longest ten

minutes that Dan Largo had ever spent. Determined not to pander to Elinora Langford, he waited twenty minutes before knocking on her bedroom door. When she opened the door, her cheeks were coloured by anger that matched perfectly the scarlet silk night dress she wore; a night dress that was intended to hide no secrets, and did not. She quickly shed her annoyance at being kept waiting.

'Do come in, Dan,' she breathed.

Largo now knew what a fly must feel like before the spider gobbled him up.

She yawned.

'Why, I almost dozed off waiting.'

As he passed her on his way into the room, she craftily narrowed the angle of passage so that he had to brush against her.

Kerosene on fire.

He was not at all sure that he could go through with his plan to tease Elinora Langford, and then leave cock-a-hoop.

She lingered near him on her way to

pour drinks from a crystal decanter.

More kerosene. Lots more fire.

Largo had to admit that, as a stoker, Elinora Langford was a mighty talented woman. The touch of her fingers on his as she handed him his drink lingered for just the perfect time.

'Cheers,' she said, sipping the brandy which was her preferred beverage. Her pouted lips played with the rim of the crystal glass.

More kerosene.

Inferno!

★   ★   ★

The bedside lamp fluttered, its flame teased by the stiffish breeze that had come up and was blowing through the open bedroom window. Largo lay on his back, a man satisfied in all respects. Elinora Langford lay with her head on his naked chest, still heaving from the exertions of trying to keep up with her athleticism and inventiveness. A yellow moon, what folk around

Spicer's Crossing called a Mississippi moon, hung in the sky above the town, its benign face mottled by scudding storm clouds. Ghostly shadows danced on the bedroom walls, and sometimes crept sinisterly across the floor towards the bed.

'Happy, Dan?' Elinora Langford murmured huskily.

'Yep,' Largo replied drowsily.

Elinora let a moment pass. She had worked hard. He had almost been persuaded. But not quite.

'Dan, about Skull Pass?'

'The answer's the same, Elinora. I'm not going with you to Skull Pass.'

Bewildered, she said, 'But I thought . . . '

He raised himself on to one elbow and looked down into her face.

'If it's any consolation, Elinora,' he told her. 'All this wining and dining and bedding almost worked.'

He hurried from the room, one leg in his trousers, feeling the bump on his skull where a crystal scent bottle had scored a direct hit. As he made his way along the hall to his own room, articles still smashed and crashed in Elinora Langford's room, proving that she was a lady of hot and long-lasting temper.

Entering his room, he fell heavily onto the bed, but not from exhaustion. No, sir. When he woke up, he had a second bump on his skull, this time, he figured, from the butt of a six-gun. He quickly checked his wallet. He had not been robbed. So what had been the purpose of his being rendered unconscious, if it was not to be robbed?

Ed Baldwin came to mind, sneaking up on a man to take his revenge would be his style. Discounting the bump on his skull, he was injury-free. Would Baldwin have missed his chance to kick him half to death? The more he thought about it, the less sense his waylaying made.

Considering it an incident not worthy of prolonged attention, it was a mystery quickly forgotten. Eager to shake the town's dust from him, Dan Largo put the matter from his mind. Western towns and what happened in them could take up a man's entire life trying to figure them out, and two lifetimes correcting wrongs, real or perceived.

He shaved, dressed in trail clothes, noticing as he did the loss of his favourite and lucky silk neck-tie that was part of his gambling duds. He went downstairs to the dining-room for breakfast, and then on to the livery to collect his horse. He hung the valise in which he carried his gambling duds on his saddle-horn and, ready to depart, found his way blocked by Ed Baldwin, his stocky frame filling the livery gate. His right cheek, where Largo's gun-barrel had raked across it, was a dirty yellow with a black tinge that was spreading steadily towards his swollen nose. His right eye was a black pebble in the swollen face.

Baldwin touched his injured cheek.

'You'll be paying for this, Largo.'

'Can't see how, seeing that I'm riding out with no intention of ever coming back this way.'

'You'll still be paying,' he snorted. 'You'll see.'

Making no sense of the lawman's remarks, figuring that the blow to his face must have shook his brain as well, he rode on along Main, headed south out of town. Doc Lonergan came to his office door to say goodbye.

'Watch your back for a spell, Largo,' he warned. 'Rupe Lambert was mighty het-up when he left here a while back. Thought he'd blast Baldwin, until the sheriff said something that calmed him down.'

'Thanks for the warning, Doc,' Largo said. 'Maybe we'll meet again around a blackjack table.'

'Maybe.' The medico chuckled. 'Though I'd prefer a little less excitement the next time.'

Elinora Langford was at her bedroom window as he rode past. He tipped his hat, but she turned away. You know, Dan Largo, he told himself, riding into Skull Pass might be a small price to pay for that woman's charms.

He sighed regretfully. 'Bye, Elinora honey.'

Scowling darkly, Ed Baldwin watched Largo ride away.

Once the curiosity surrounding the gambler's departure died down and folk went back to going about their business, Baldwin hurriedly made his way to a stand of trees on the fringe of town where he had a saddled horse waiting. Not wanting to attract curious eyes, with the deed he had planned, he made tracks on a circuitous route that would eventually cross Dan Largo's trail at a creek about five miles outside town. He had planned his stealthy departure with grim purpose, and as he rode he took pleasure in knowing that his revenge on the gambler would be sweeter than wild honey. He massaged his violated right cheek, and consoled himself with the thought that Largo's punishment would be of a permanent nature.

2

It was a pleasant morning, the wind soft, and still holding the coolness of the Fall night. It would be a short respite. Soon the breeze would slacken and the air would pick up the fire from the desert country to the south, and a man's lungs would burn with each oxygen-starved breath. But for now, Largo, a man who spent a whole lot of time in smoke-filled saloons dealing cards, would enjoy the invigoratingly refreshing air.

It was unfamiliar country to Dan Largo, his visit to Spicer's Crossing being his first and last. In fact he was not a frequent visitor anywhere. He had long since decided that roots were not for him, and therefore lived the life of an itinerant. His patience soon wore thin in a new town, and once he had taken a couple of poker or blackjack pots, he was ready to hit the trail again; a trail that never specifically led anywhere, and only ended when it reached a town where there was a card game to sit in on. The mystery as to where his next stop might be had always added spice to his wanderings. He had travelled most trails west of the Mississippi, and some others too. But the country was so vast that he could ride forever and not visit a fraction of its town and cities.

Idly ambling along, his thoughts turned to Elinora Langford, and for the first time since the night before, while languishing in Elinora's arms, he thought about roots. The idea had come as quite a shock to him the previous night, he not figuring on ever having himself tied to apron strings — not that he could ever imagine the beautiful Elinora Langford in an apron. Where had she come from? He realized that he knew nothing about her. What kind of woman was she really? Why the hell did she want to go to this place that her Uncle Willie had called Skull Pass, of all places?

These were some of the questions he had had in mind to ask the night before, but had curbed his curiosity, feeling that the more he knew about Elinora Langford, the more intrigued and mezmerized by her he would become; and a woman, even the spirited type like Elinora, slowed a man down until he finally stopped. The fact was that he was not a man who took easily to domesticity, preferring to be footloose and fancy-free. Even if he had found a woman who was prepared to go from town to town with him, following the trail of a gambling man, it would not last and it would not be fair. Women, he reckoned, however they might protest to the contrary, were homemakers by nature and instinct.

Coming out of a stretch of spruce, Largo observed that the trail criss-crossed another narrower and, by the look of its shaggy state of repair, less-frequented trail. A shady creek sat at the cross of the trail and made a natural resting place, offering a sloping bank to lie on and a sandy hollow where a man could start a decent fire. The creek's water was as clear as a sparkling diamond and tempted Largo to drink and fill his canteen. He froze on hearing a six-gun being cocked.

Ed Baldwin's warning throbbed with menace.

'Move and I'll blast you Largo! Drop the Peacemaker in the creek.'

Largo cursed silently. He should have been prepared for what had happened. He had read Baldwin wrong. He had figured that the sheriff would crawl away and hide until his shame at having been pistol-whipped would no longer be the topic of conversation. He should have counted on all worms turning one day.

'Do it!' Baldwin screamed, his tone high-pitched with hysterical rage. 'And ease your damn gun out of its holster with two fingers only.'

Largo, not being a man with a

choice, did as he had been told. He grimaced as the Peacemaker plonked into the creek and lay glistening in the clear water, useless now, even if he could get to it.

'Stand up! Don't turn 'round!' the sheriff barked.

'Going to shoot me in the back, Baldwin?' Largo asked. 'Must say that with a cur like you, I wouldn't expect it to be any other way.'

'I ain't going to shoot you, Largo,' the tainted lawman said smugly. 'I've got much more interestin' plans for you, mister.'

He whistled. From the trees high on the bank overlooking the creek a rider emerged, and it took Dan Largo no time at all to recognize Rupe Lambert's gait. Largo now knew what Baldwin had meant when he'd said that he'd pay. He had clearly arranged with Rupe Lambert to extract payment in double measure.

'Hoping to get back in Rupe Lambert's good books, Sheriff?' Largo taunted. 'So that he won't tell his old man about your lackadaisical handling of the events in town that left him dragging a leg?'

'Shut your mouth!' Baldwin raged.

Ed Baldwin would know that, though Horatio Lonergan had inflicted Rupe Lambert's thigh wound, Charles Lambert would understand the medico's necessary action to keep his son breathing. However, he would not forgive Baldwin. Charles Lambert would have expected Largo to have paid heavily for what had happened, and he'd have expected Baldwin to be the deliverer of that punishment. That he had not been, would earn Charles Lambert's swift and harsh retribution.

'Still yellow through and through, Baldwin,' Largo again taunted the sheriff. 'Hadn't the spunk to face me yourself, huh?'

Baldwin's grin was leeringly evil.

'This is going to be a day full of surprises, Largo.'

He addressed the man splashing

across the creek.

'Howdy, Rupe. Didn't keep you waitin' too long, I hope?'

Rupe Lambert drew rein in front of Dan Largo.

'Pleasure is always worth waiting for, Ed.'

He dismounted and stood facing Largo: fists balled, mouth mean, face contorted with the rage that burned in his gut.

'Grab him!' he ordered the sheriff.

He promised Largo, 'I'm going to beat you senseless, mister!'

A couple of seconds later, his hot-tempered question was addressed to Baldwin.

'What're you waiting for? Hold the bastard!'

Baldwin sneered.

'Well, now, Rupe. You see, I didn't tell you all of my plan when I jawed with you at the doc's office this morning . . . '

'Huh? Lambert grunted. 'What the hell are you guffing about?'

Ed Baldwin took on the tone a school teacher might when trying to explain a ticklish problem to a dumb-skulled pupil. When he spoke, his voice held sarcasm and contempt in about equal measure.

'You see, Rupe — '

'What the hell's gotten into you, Ed?' Lambert growled. 'You going to hold Largo or not?'

'No.'

'No?' Lambert asked, stunned.

'That's what I said,' Baldwin replied.

'What devil's game are you playing at, Baldwin?' Lambert snarled.

Dan Largo's laughter got Rupe Lambert's full attention.

'You know, I believe I've been reading you wrong, Sheriff.'

'You're a smart fella, that I'll give you, Largo,' Baldwin said.

'Will someone tell me what's being hatched here?' Rupe Lambert growled.

'You'll correct me if I'm wrong, won't you, Baldwin?' Largo said.

'Sure will.'

Largo told a bemused Lambert.

'Well, I figure that the sheriff here wants me sitting pretty in his jail, waiting for your old man to come riding in and pat him on the back for apprehending his son's murderer. How am I doing, Sheriff?'

'You're doing ace,' Baldwin confirmed.

Largo turned back to an even more bemused Rupe Lambert.

'You see, I figure the sheriff reckons he's on to a skinning from your pa for what happened back in town. He would have wanted him to at least whup me good, if not string me up. Now, I think that our skunk lawman here doesn't want to take a chance on bearing the brunt of your pa's fury.'

Largo turned to Baldwin.

'Want me to go on, Sheriff? Or would you prefer to tell Lambert why he's really here?'

Rupe Lambert's puzzled gaze settled on the Spicer's Crossing lawman.

'What's he gabbing about, Ed?'

Baldwin shrugged in response to Largo's question. 'I reckon you're doing just dandy, gambler.'

Rupe Lambert's hand dived for his gun. 'You tell me what's brewing right now, Baldwin. Or so help me — '

Ed Baldwin's gun exploded, and a ragged hole appeared in Rupe Lambert's wrist.

'I guess you're getting the picture, huh, Lambert?' Dan Largo said.

As he backed away, cowering under the threat of Baldwin's tracking Colt, it was clear that he had indeed got the picture.

'No, Ed,' he whined.

Again the sheriff shrugged, his expression devoid of the least modicum of pity for the cringing man.

'Don't have a choice, Rupe. Largo, foxy gent that he is, told the story good. He's right. Your old man would skin me alive.'

His eyes became dreamy.

'You see, Rupe, I've spent twenty years dodging trouble to plank my butt on a porch-rocker. I took real grief and ate a mess of humble-pie during that time, but I figured it was worth it to get to sit and watch sunsets with the comfort of a sheriff's pension behind me.'

His face blotched with a purple anger.

'Then yesterday you rode in, prodding for trouble like you always do, you dumb-skulled bastard, figuring that any you got into would go your way, seeing who you are.'

Ed Baldwin laughed bitterly. 'Shit, Rupe. You know how many times over the years I've wanted to creep up on you in the dark and back-shoot you?

'Have you?' he yelled.

Rupe Lambert was agape at the revelation. 'Gee, I figured you for a friend, Ed,' he mumbled.

Baldwin snorted derisively.

'Just goes to show how dumb you are, Rupe. I guess you've got some kind of sickness in your brain that your pa brought home from one of those whores he liked to dally with in that high-toned cathouse the other side of the Rio Grande.'

Anger flared in Rupe Lambert's face, but its glow lasted as briefly as a match in a gale. He dropped to his knees under the threat of Baldwin's gun.

'Please, Ed,' he wailed. He held out his shattered wrist. 'I won't tell my daddy how I got this.' He then slapped his injured thigh. 'Or this neither,' he whined. 'You have my word.'

Ed Baldwin thought this was hilarious.

'Your word ain't worth diddly, Rupe. If I let you off the hook, you'll plug me in the back the second I turn 'round. And if you didn't, you'd have your pox-ridden old man heading this way with fifty men and a rope.'

He pressed the gun-barrel to Rupe Lambert's forehead.

'It's got to be this way, Rupe,' he said emotionlessly. 'The story's going to be that Largo followed you out of town. I saw him leave and hit the trail after him, figuring that he had no good intentions. Thing is, I was just a couple of minutes too late.'

The sheriff warmed to his story, proving to be a credible actor.

'I heard gunfire.'

Baldwin's slick planning came as a surprise to Dan Largo. He should have realized that to act the fool successfully, a man needed to be really smart. Largo was beginning to think that he might be getting too long in the tooth for the risk-laden life of a gambler.

'I found your body here at the creek, Rupe,' Baldwin sniggered. 'You'd struggled for your life . . . '

Smiling smugly, the sheriff took a silk neck-tie from his vest pocket and dangled it in front of Largo.

'The killer made a real bad mistake, Rupe. He left this in your grasp.'

Dan Largo now knew the purpose of Baldwin's visit to his room the night before!

'I recognized the gambler's fancy silk

neck-tie,' Baldwin continued enthusiastically. 'I guess other folk will too.' He chuckled. 'Sure hope I put a good dent on that skull of yours last night, Largo?'

He continued the tale which he figured would get him out of a bind with Charles Lambert, and put Dan Largo's neck in a hangman's noose.

Both of which were possibilities that were becoming more likely by the second, Largo thought.

Baldwin's excitement at the craftiness of his plan grew with gusto. 'Largo had let out, but I caught him up. Hauled him back to town for hangin'.' He leered evilly. 'Or anything else your old man might have in mind as a just punishment.'

Baldwin's eyes glittered like diamonds. His left hand massaged his swollen jaw.

'Maybe draggin' behind a buckboard, like he did that wrangler who stole ten bucks from him last Fall.'

The snake-crooked lawman glared at Dan Largo. 'I guess I might even suggest that as a righter of wrongs to Mr Lambert. He's a mean-minded bastard at the best of times. Buckboard-hauling is a real slow and painful way to die, Largo.'

He graphically elaborated.

'Each strip of flesh is torn from a man's body, inch by bloody inch,' he gloated dreamily. 'A man could take a long time to die that way.'

'You'll never get away with it, Baldwin,' Rupe Lambert shouted, in a brief spurt of defiance.

'Sure he will,' Largo said, and qualified, 'up to a point, anyway.'

'Oh, yeah,' the crooked lawman said. -'And what point would that be?'

'The point where I'll rip out your poisoned heart, Baldwin!' the gambler growled.

He quickly built on the flash of concern that showed in the sheriff's eyes.

'Think about it,' Largo encouraged Ed Baldwin. 'Killing Lambert's the easy part. After that you'll have to haul me back to town, slap me in jail and wait for Rupe's enraged pappy to put in an appearance. Now, as I hear it, that gent gets around. He could even be back East looking after one of his many business interests.' Dan Largo shook his head. 'It could take him quite a spell to make it to Spicer's Crossing.'

Ed Baldwin's thick tongue licked lips as dry as Mojave sand. Largo figured he might have him on the run. He stoked his fear even more.

'All those long days and nights waiting, Sheriff. Any second of which I could get the drop on you.'

Largo's icy-blue eyes bored into Baldwin. The sheriff trembled.

'Think about that,' he urged, in a funeral-hollow voice.

'He's got you wetting in your pants, Ed, ain't he?' Rupe Lambert sniggered.

Largo loaded on the menace.

'I reckon you'd never get to see that rocker you've planned for, Sheriff. One second . . . one slip . . . and . . . '

Largo graphically drew a finger

across his throat.

Flushed with new hope, Rupe Lambert became positively swaggerish and repeated Dan Largo's action with a cruel, slashing flourish. Then he began clutching at his imaginary slit throat, gagging.

A shudder went through Baldwin.

'And you've forgotten something really important, Sheriff,' the gambler said.

Ed Baldwin's eyes darted, like a trapped animal.

'Yeah? What?' he croaked.

'Doc Lonergan's testimony,' Largo informed him.

Panic gripped Baldwin.

'Seems to me that the doc's word might be really important to Charles Lambert.'

'Yeah,' Rupe Lambert enthused. 'That's so, Baldwin. My old man thinks a whole lot of the doc. They became really friendly when he saved his life after he was bushwhacked a coupla years back.'

Clearly, Baldwin had not counted on Horatio Lonergan's influence with Charles Lambert.

'I suggest you forget this whole thing, Sheriff,' Dan Largo casually proposed. 'Take Rupe's word about him not telling his pa about events. With any luck, by the time he meets up with his old man his wounds will have healed anyway.'

'I'll ride to Mexico. Rest up for a spell,' Lambert offered. 'By the time I meet my daddy again, I'll be as good as new.'

Like a trapped animal seeking a safe escape route, Ed Baldwin considered his options with increasing agitation.

'Let this be an end to this affair, Sheriff Baldwin,' the gambler cajoled. 'Let Lambert and me ride on about our business.'

'Yeah,' Lambert coaxed. 'No hard feelings, Ed.'

'Sensible, I'd say,' Largo told the wavering lawman.

Dan Largo reckoned he'd snared

Baldwin when, out of the blue, the lawman's grit was restored and his smile again became cocky.

'I've got a better idea, gents.'

Dan Largo had the sinking feeling that, as far as Ed Baldwin went, he had made his third and probably final mistake.

'Well now,' Baldwin began in a strutting manner, 'smart as Largo's plan is, I figure I've got an even foxier one.'

His laughter was mocking; the laughter of a man who had his enemies nailed.

'I'm going to kill you both!'

Dan Largo's sinking feeling had been well justified.

3

Explaining the guts of his new scheme, Ed Baldwin was in an expansionary mood.

'The plan can be the same up to where you catch it, Rupe. But now, Largo being such a threat to my health, I have no choice but to sink lead in him.'

Pleased as a well-pleasured man, the sheriff became positively exuberant.

'I'll sling you both on your horses and ride back to town, quite the hero, I figure. Lonergan's word won't matter none. I'll be the only witness to what happened here.'

Dan Largo found himself having a sneaking feeling of admiration for the lawman's foxiness.

'Largo?' Rupe Lambert panicked. 'Ain't you got any ideas?'

The gambler sighed.

'I'm fresh out, Lambert.'

Without further fuss, Ed Baldwin squeezed the Colt's trigger and most of Rupe Lambert's face and head vanished in a splurge of red. Part of his skull plopped into the creek, its attached hair bobbing in the rippling brook for a second before sinking beneath the water, leaving behind a trailing red stain that widened as other skull fragments joined the first.

Largo had seen many a cruel act in his time, but none so cruel and calculating as what he had just witnessed. The killing was the act of a terrified man, and therefore a man more dangerous than the wildest beast. Ed Baldwin would perpetrate the most heinous crime, rather than risk losing what he had planned to possess.

In the blink of an eye, Baldwin's gun was on Largo. The gambler, though used to violence in the towns and territories he'd been through, was caught flat-footed by the swiftness of Rupe Lambert's execution, and had forfeited the split-second in which he might have lunged at the twisted lawman. The chance wasted, he was totally at Baldwin's mercy, and there wouldn't be any mercy shown.

'I guess we won't be needing this now.' Baldwin tossed Largo's neck-tie into the creek and watched it float away. 'No call for it to be found in Rupe Lambert's clenched fist, now that I got the drop on you right in the act of killing him.'

The sheriff speculated, 'You know, Largo, being a hero might bring me a fat poke. I hear, to those who serve him well, Charles Lambert is a mighty generous cuss.'

As the killer-sheriff levelled his gun on Dan Largo, the gambler knew he should be settling accounts for the hereafter, but, hell, all he could think about was Elinora Langford and the pleasures that her soft, warm, pliable body had given him the previous night, and the homely instincts she had induced in him, from which he'd run like a chicken chased by a fox. He wondered if he had chosen differently, would Elinora Langford have turned out to be the woman who would have finally tamed him?

Now he would never know.

The trigger of Ed Baldwin's Colt had a whisper to go when a rifle shot punched a hole right between his eyes, snatching his right eye from its socket. His finger jerked on the pistol's trigger, forcing Largo to lean aside as a ball of orange flame left the Colt's barrel, headed in his direction. Baldwin's bullet whizzed past, fanning his left cheek with its breeze, and thudded into the stout trunk of a gnarled spruce behind him, spitting back a chunk of the tree's bark that buzzed through the air over his head.

Not knowing who was shooting from the scrub on a knoll where the creek flowed past a wooded slope, Largo dived for Ed Baldwin's pistol. He belly-rolled into a dip between twin boulders, gun cocked, ready and seeking. The likelihood was that the rifleman was a friend, but he might also be just a lousy shooter who had plugged Baldwin in error. He'd made enough mistakes and errors of judgement for one day, without adding to his tally.

'Show yourself!' he called out.

The scrub stirred and parted. 'You going to stay cringing behind those boulders all day, Dan?' Elinora Langford enquired. 'Want me to come hold your hand, maybe?'

He stood up, his ears pushed back by a grin as wide as the Rio Grande, and chirped cheekily 'I've got more interesting things you could be holding, Elinora honey.'

She flung back, every bit as cheekily, 'It's only interesting when those things are a secret, Dan. After last night you've got no secrets from me!'

'Isn't that a fact,' he laughed.

He slung his arm around Elinora Langford's waist and hauled her to him, letting not even air between them. His lips closed on hers and landed on her left cheek as she averted her head. Then, with surprising strength she pushed him away, loftily admonishing him.

'Saving your hide doesn't give any other privileges, Mr Largo.'

'Oh, come on, Elinora I know you're just itching for some more of what we had last night.'

As he drew her to him again, she wedged the barrel of her rifle between his legs, pointed upwards. Dan Largo chuckled. Hell! Elinora Langford was one spirited woman!

His thoughts were interrupted by the clatter of a rock hurtling down the spruce-clad slope on the far side of the creek. Largo spun around, gun cocked. Instinctively he offered his protection to Elinora, thinking how damn chivalrous he'd become all of a sudden. It was something that worried him greatly. Was Elinora Langford becoming that important to him?

'Don't shoot, Mr Largo,' an as-yet unseen man whined. 'Don't mean no harm to you and Miss Langford.'

'Show yourself!' Largo ordered the man.

A small, weedy man, with wispy fair hair and frightened bulging eyes stepped from the trees, hands high, holding the reins of his nag. Largo recognized the hotel clerk, who the night before had delivered a bottle of champagne to Elinora's room. His name was Andy White. He tried to ignore Rupe Lambert's and Ed Baldwin's bodies, but his fear-filled eyes kept darting in their direction.

'I saw nothin', Mr Largo,' he whined, terrified. 'I was just passin' by on my way to my sister's cabin a little ways on.'

'It was a mighty ghostly passage, mister,' Largo said, quietly. To the hearer, menacingly.

'I won't say a single word, Mr La-Largo,' the snivelling hotel clerk stuttered. 'Honest, I won't.'

The gambler's gaze took in the two bodies on the ground. 'As a matter of interest. What kind of words were you thinking of saying?'

The last vestige of blood drained from the hotel clerk's face, and though his mouth opened and closed no words came forth, only a tortured, whimpering sound.

'Ride on, mister,' Largo said tiredly.

'You mean it?' Andy White bleated.

Largo nodded.

'Th-thanks, Mr La-Largo,' he stammered, scrambling into the saddle. 'Not one word,' he promised again, before vanishing into the trees.

'You believe him?' Elinora Langford asked.

'Not for a second,' he replied.

'Then why the hell did you let him go?' she challenged hotly.

'What else was there to do?' Largo asked, every bit as hotly. His gaze locked with hers, and he was stunned. 'You'd have killed him?'

'It's a matter of survival and self-protection, Dan,' she said matter-of-factly. 'He'll ride back to town faster than the wind to tell them we murdered Rupe Lambert and the sheriff.'

'Which makes it all the more urgent that we get there first with our story, doesn't it?' he growled. 'So let's get these hoboes' bodies on their horses and ride.'

'We'd be better off making tracks, Dan,' Elinora Langford opined.

'Maybe to Skull Pass?'

Elinora Langford's come-hither smile, the gambler reckoned, must have got men to do a whole lot they might not normally do, and if he were not careful, he'd find himself included in what he figured was a mighty sizeable outfit.

'I'm headed back to town,' he announced determinedly. 'You make tracks wherever you want, Elinora.'

'You disappoint me, Dan Largo,' she flared angrily.

'I guess I do, Elinora,' he replied with a heavy sigh. 'But you see, I'm a man who likes to keep a clean slate. If I make tracks now, I'm going to have the law dogging my trail for quite a spell.

Best to set the record straight.'

Elinora Langford was shaking her head as if he were a kid caught with his hand in the cookie jar.

'You go back to town, Dan, and they'll sling a rope over the nearest tree.'

Largo considered her statement for a spell.

'Elinora, if we had a chance to get to know each other a little better, you'd find that I'm a tidy-minded sort of fella, who likes a simple life.'

'Your choice, Dan,' she vaulted into the saddle of the fiery-blooded stallion she rode. 'But I figure that this simple life you're so keen on will be short-lived once you arrive back in Spicer's Crossing. Ed Baldwin wasn't much of a sheriff or a man, but he was *their* sheriff. Towns I've been through get pretty het-up about people, particularly gamblers,' she emphasized pointedly, 'who go and kill their lawman.'

She shook her head as if she were dealing with the fool of all fools.

'They'll string you up for sure.'

'I didn't kill Baldwin, Elinora!'

She ignored his feistily-delivered protest.

'It won't matter, Dan. You're a stranger; a gambler. Who are they going to believe? You or one of their own?'

She had put forward a good case that made a whole lot of sense. Largo felt his feet on shifting sands.

Elinora Langford continued with her reasoning. 'Now, even if they were to overlook the gunning of their sheriff, Dan, they certainly won't look the other way when you drop Rupe Lambert's body on their doorstep. They'll be thinking about the kind of wrath that Charles Lambert will unleash on the town.'

She leaned forward on her saddle-horn, offering a view of her bountiful breasts to Largo's gaze. He might have his neck almost in a noose, but he was still alive and kicking where it mattered to a man.

'Now. I reckon the town will figure

that a body *for a body* is a fair trade to placate Charles Lambert, Dan.'

She wheeled the stallion, ready to depart.

'Where are you headed, Elinora?' Largo found himself asking, despite having resolved only a second before to let her ride away without another word exchanged. Damn! He was beginning to worry about the woman's welfare, and he knew that that was a sure sign that Elinora Langford was beginning to mean more to him than he wanted her to.

What was it about the woman that drew him to her like a moth to a flame? She was beautiful, sure enough, but he'd bedded beautiful women before. There was that rancher's daughter only a week ago, he recalled pleasantly. But he'd always been able to walk away when he wanted to. He wasn't at all sure that he could do that with Elinora Langford, and that was a real crux.

'To the next town or saloon where I'll find a man to take me to Skull Pass. Or whatever the damn name of the place is,' she replied testily.

'Why're you so hell-bent on having that mane of red hair dangling on a Apache scalp-pole?' he asked frustratedly.

'No risk, no gain, Dan.'

'What kind of gain would warrant riding into Skull Pass?' he wanted to know.

'Treasure,' she stated simply.

'Treasure, huh?'

'Big treasure,' she baited. 'Really big treasure, Dan.'

She purred like the devil must have whispered in Eve's ear in the Garden of Eden, when she got a hankering for apples. Temptation coursed through the gambler with the fury of a mountain torrent when the winter snows melted.

'Just sitting there for you and me to pick it up,' Elinora Langford coaxed, her green eyes dancing with all sorts of promise.

Observing Largo's crumbling resolve, her voice took on a husky vibrancy that had Largo's heart racing, fit to leap out of his mouth.

'We could head for South America? Europe? Maybe London? Always had a hankering to see London, Dan.' Her mood became positively skittish. 'Paris!'

Satan was curling his tail around Largo and dragging him towards probable damnation.

'There are lots of gambling halls in London and Paris,' she tempted. 'Places where a card-handy *hombre* like you could make a fortune in no time at all.'

Largo grabbed hold of his last vestige of resolve.

'Stop it right there, Elinora!' he commanded her spiritedly. 'I'm headed back to town to set the record straight. Then on to the next town where there's a card game. You ride along with me, if you want.'

There! He'd tied his wagon to Elinora Langford's, if she had a mind to tie hers to his.

Maybe she could change his mind along the way, she speculated. She had changed mens' minds before. Dan Largo would prove to be a tougher proposition, of course. Maybe the town would believe his story after all? Her dreaming did not last more than a couple of seconds. There would be no *along the way*. If they returned to town, there wasn't a chance in hell of them riding away from Spicer's Crossing.

She restated this view to the gambler.

'They'll stretch your fool neck for sure.' She urged the stallion forward. 'Bye, Dan.'

He watched her leave with a heavy heart, but his resolve to clean his slate held — despite his desire to charge after Elinora Langford.

'Good luck,' he wished her. 'Just a word of advice, Elinora. Don't you go telling every bar-room swiller about that treasure.'

'I'm not *loco*, Dan,' she smiled.

'You told me,' he reminded her.

'You,' she said with a sad smile, 'I trust.'

He watched her into the trees from

where the hotel clerk had made his appearance a couple of minutes earlier until she was out of sight, every second fighting the urge to gallop after her. He told himself that once the fire in his belly died down, he'd see the sense of a decision that, right then, made no sense at all.

Wearily, he retrieved the Peacemaker from the creek, dried it off, shed its ruined loads and replaced them with fresh rounds. He then put Baldwin and Rupe Lambert's bodies onboard their horses and led the grim procession out of the creek and along the trail back to town — looking back more often than he looked forward.

4

Andy White's charge along the main street of Spicer's Crossing had doors opening. Like other Western towns being tamed by the coming of law and order excitement was waning, and days in the main, dragged uneventfully by.

Life in the town, being within spitting distance of the border, had not always been so sedate, and had had in the not-too-distant past, (the good old days, as folk who had not suffered their cruelty would have it) more than its fair share of bust-ups. The regular visits of US marshals and no-nonsense judges, as law and order took hold, had put the run under most of the hard cases who used to frequent Spicer's Crossing. The only buckers of law and order now were the die-hards, whose list of atrocities put them well out of reach of any sympathy. They were no-hopers who would eventually end up on the wrong end of a marshal's gun or a judge's rope.

The fast-exit trails to Mexico had grown quieter. A sign of tamed times was the closure of the town's last whorehouse a couple of months previously, while its only saloon was just staying afloat. The hotel, too, had more empty than occupied rooms.

White's frenzied gallop was the kind of charge that not long ago would have had strollers diving for cover. When he drew rein, he was immediately surrounded by curious citizens flinging questions at him.

'It's that gambler,' he said breathlessly, not having drawn a full breath since his clash with Dan Largo twenty minutes before. 'He's murdered Ed Baldwin.'

He followed that statement up with even more stunning news.

'Rupe Lambert, too.'

Though the murder of their sheriff had shocked his listeners, the news of

Rupe Lambert's demise had them reeling. No one would really miss Ed Baldwin, but there would be a hell of a price extracted by Charles Lambert for his son's death.

Shock followed shock.

'The woman . . . Elinora Langford . . . '

Breaths were held.

Enjoying the limelight, the hotel clerk drew the last vestige of suspense from his story.

'She was in it with that damn gambler.'

This news got a cool, unbelieving reception. Elinora Langford had made a favourable impression on the men of Spicer's Crossing, some had even put her on a pedestal. None of them wanted to believe that she could have such malice in her.

'I saw her do it,' White hurriedly lied, anxious to avoid any probing questions which might reveal that all he'd heard was a series of shots. By the time he had arrived on the scene, Rupe

Lambert and Ed Baldwin were already dead. White figured, not unreasonably so from his point of view, that Lambert and Baldwin having always been cosy with each other, the only conclusion that could be drawn from what he'd witnessed was that Largo and Langford had done the deed of murder.

'You saw them kill Lambert and Baldwin, Andy?'

White spun around to face Doc Lonergan. He was beginning to realize that he'd dug himself into a hole by his wild, unsubstantiated claims. Pulling back from the pit that he'd opened up would make him look a fool.

He repeated his lie.

'Sure did.' And to stymie any other questions said, 'I was right there when them hell-cats pulled the trigger.'

Not a man normally given to telling tall tales, the crowd took the hotel clerk's word. Horatio Lonergan was the exception to the rule, understanding that a man as insignificant as Andy White would find it hard to walk away from being the centre of attention. He did not believe that he would lie intentionally; rather he believed that he was making a mountain out of a molehill.

'We gotta get a posse ridin',' a russet-haired, mean-eyed man called Spence Waterman declared. Waterman had been a minor gunfighter who, recognizing his limitations with an iron, had taken to grabbing any trouble-stirring opportunities presented to him.

He stepped forward from the pack. 'Who's with me?'

The uptake on his invitation was at first sluggish. Posses got men killed.

'You fellas want Charles Lambert asking why we sat on our duffs and did nothing?' Waterman growled.

The prospect of that happening focused the men's attention. A sizeable posse was soon lined up on Main, ready to ride, when they were stopped dead in their tracks by the appearance of Dan Largo riding in, Baldwin's and Lambert's bodies in tow.

Waterman was first to find his voice.

'Looks like we don't have to trouble ourselves friends. The fly is walkin' right into our parlour.'

'If he's killed Baldwin and Lambert,' one of the posse pondered, 'why'd he want to do that, Spence?'

'Don't make much sense to me,' another of the posse added. 'Largo ridin' freely to a noose.'

'Maybe he figures there isn't going to be a noose waiting, Joey,' Doc Lonergan suggested, in answer to the last man's speculation.

'That's crazy talk, Doc,' Spence Waterman spat, sour because he had been robbed of running a man to ground, a pastime he liked. 'Any murderer must expect to be strung up.'

'Yes,' the medico readily agreed. 'If he's a murderer. But what if the man isn't a murderer? What if he's just doing the decent thing, delivering back the bodies of the men who had challenged him to their rightful place?' Stumped for a moment, Waterman quickly recovered to dampen Lonergan's speculations. His smile was leery.

'Ain't you forgettin' that Andy White saw Largo and that she-cat Elinora Langford murder those fine men, Doc?'

'I'm not forgetting.'

Lonergan sought out the hotel clerk in the crowd. Finding him, White flinched under the medico's steely gaze. Other eyes followed Lonergan's. Andy White began to sweat. If he changed his story now, he'd be the one lynched! He had no choice but to stick steadfastly to his lying.

'I did, too,' he chanted, brazen-faced.

Waterman was smug. 'Good 'nuff for you, Doc?'

The crowd went Waterman's way. Lonergan's protests were shouted down.

Making his way along Main, confronted by a howling mob, Dan Largo began having doubts about the wisdom of having put in an appearance. The mounted men had the look of a posse. Elinora Langford might have called it right, at that.

He drew rein. His horse, sensing the hostile mood, fought the reins. 'Easy, boy,' he coaxed the frightened animal.

It was a stand-off!

A hush fell. Menace grew. Largo let his hand drift towards the Peacemaker on his right hip.

The tense impasse was broken when a man called Gus Reilly, a fellow close in ilk to Spence Waterman, fierily accused, 'Stinkin' murderer!'

Dan Largo had no more doubts. Elinora Langford had been right. He had indeed put his neck in a noose!

Any chance of making a run for it vanished a second later.

'I got the murderin' bastard covered!'

Dan Largo's spine chilled when he heard the shotgun behind him being cocked.

'Grab him!' Waterman ordered the men on either side of him. He instructed another man, a sidekick of his, whose eyes were glistening with the excitement of a lynching, 'Sling a rope, Ned. That oak near the livery should do just dandy.'

'Sure thing, Spence,' Ned laughed, hyena-like.

He grabbed a lariat from a nearby horse and ran to the appointed oak to loop the rope over its stoutest branch. He tugged on the rope to take up the slack and tested its tautness.

'Ready when you fellas are,' he called back, repeating his hyena laugh.

If he could reach his own arse with his boot, Dan Largo would have kicked himself.

'I didn't murder anyone,' he proclaimed resolutely, hoping that someone with sense would pick up on the ring of truth in his declaration. His hostile gaze came to rest on Andy White. 'Any man who says I did, is a skunk liar!'

The hotel clerk took refuge in the surging crowd.

As the men charged forward, Dan Largo fumed at his helplessness. If he went for his gun the shotgun-toter behind him would be only too thrilled to cut him down. And if he did nothing, he would be hauled from his horse and marched to the hanging tree. It was a no-win predicament that he'd got himself into.

Elinora honey, he growled to himself, I should have listened to your good advice.

He was pulled from his horse and dragged towards the oak. All he could hope for now was a miracle, and those he did not believe in. It looked like Spicer's Crossing was the end of the trail for him.

5

Doc Lonergan stepped forward. Not that his intervention would make one iota of difference, Largo figured.

'Wait. Every man deserves a fair trial.'

'Not a cold-blooded killer the likes of this honcho,' Waterman rejected.

Led by Waterman, a bunch of men continued to drag Dan Largo relentlessly to the waiting rope. The Doc's attempts to stop the lynch mob proving futile, it looked like he was going to end up swinging in the breeze.

'Lynching is against the law, men,' Lonergan tried in vain.

'There ain't no law,' Waterman chanted. 'You're mind is wandering, Doc. Largo killed the sheriff, remember?'

Horatio Lonergan looked to the men who had hung back from involvement in the proceedings, but they turned away. He could understand. For example there was Don Lane, owner of the general store dependent on the lynchers' custom to remain in business. And there was Andy Bright, who owned the hardware store and was equally dependent. Besides, if they earned Charles Lambert's disapproval, he'd see to it that not a single cent would jangle their cash registers.

Though Lonergan understood, he did not approve of the men's action. In his book there were things, such as a man standing against injustice, more important than mere economic survival. Didn't they understand that a lynching demeaned their town? Once unleashed, mob law had a voracious appetite. He said as much to the men he hoped would stand with him against the outbreak of lawlessness, but his words fell on deaf ears.

'Sorry, Horatio,' Don Lane apologized. 'There's nothing we can do to stop them.'

'That's the way it is,' Andy Bright

agreed. 'Heck, Doc I'm not even sure which end a bullet comes from a gun. We're storekeepers, Horatio.'

'Stay out of it,' Lane advised Lonergan. 'The mood this town is in, you could partner that gambler.'

The medico knew the truth of Lane's statement. But, being a man of high principle, he could not let Dan Largo or any man meet his Maker unjustly and before his natural time.

He stood firmly in the mob's path.

'Get out of the way, Doc,' Waterman snarled.

Lonergan held his ground, despite the shiver in his gut at the snarling faces lined up against him.

'There'll be no lynching,' he declared. 'Unless it's over my dead body.'

A shot rang out and Lonergan buckled as he clutched his side. A sour-pussed man who spent his days in drunken blackouts, or working his way towards his next trip to oblivion, stepped from the crowd, smoke trickling from the barrel of an aged Dragoon Colt; a relic from his days in Rebel grey.

'That can be arranged, Doc,' he mocked, and then added, 'Now get outa the way you old fool!'

'Do as he says,' Largo advised the medico. 'No sense in two of us swinging. But I thank you for your concern, sir.'

The crowd surged forward then, brushing aside Lonergan's feeble efforts to stop them. Right ahead, the hanging tree loomed large, and Largo's eyes became riveted to the dangling rope. He fought to avoid it getting around his neck, but held and helpless, there was little he could do against overwhelming odds.

'Someone get a horse!' Waterman hollered. There was no shortage of willing hands, and Waterman ended up having four horses to choose from. 'Tie his hands.'

This done, he picked the surliest of the quartet of horses presented to him, a mean-tempered stallion. Three men hoisted Largo in to the saddle. He kicked out and had the pleasure of seeing his boot flatten Waterman's nose. A second kick took off the tip of another man's ear.

Snarling, Waterman screamed, 'Hang the bastard!'

The man who'd lost the tip of his ear slapped the stallion's rump. The horse bucked and took off. The rope's slackness was eaten up by the horse's mad sprint. Largo was yanked out of the saddle, and left swinging. His shoulder muscles burned at the effort of holding his weight, but they wouldn't be tortured for long. He gasped for air as the noose tightened around his neck, squeezing his windpipe.

He was not too aware of the bullet that cut the rope and sent him crashing to the ground, but he was surely grateful to the interventionist. The crowd spun around to find themselves looking into the barrel of Elinora Langford's smoking Winchester.

'Easy now, gents!'

She blasted the toe cap off the first man's boot to lunge for her. He cut loose with a agonized howl. Blood spurted from his mangled foot.

'Drop the shotgun!' Elinora ordered the blunderbuss-toter, and warned, 'The next man gets it right between the eyes.'

No one was prepared beyond that point to test the veracity of her statement.

'Cut him loose, Doc,' Elinora told Horatio Lonergan.

The medico limped forward.

'It'll be my pleasure, Miss Langford.'

On his feet and heaving air into his lungs, Dan Largo croaked. 'Left it a touch late, didn't you, Elinora honey?'

With a wry smile, she admitted, 'I could have intervened before now. But I figured that the more of the lesson you learned, the less prone you would be to making the same mistake again.'

The gambler massaged the red and purple rope-circle around his neck.

'I guess I've learned good, Elinora. Where did you learn to shoot like that?'

'Spent a stint with a travelling show as a sharp-shooter.'

Largo shook his head in wonder.

'You're one talented lady, Elinora,' he complimented.

Elinora Langford addressed the mob.

'We'll be leaving now. But before we go, I want to state categorically that neither Dan Largo or I killed Rupe Lambert or Ed Baldwin.'

She turned to Largo.

'Fill them in on the details, Dan.'

'You know, Elinora,' he grinned. 'You're a real bossy skirt.'

'Tell them how it was,' she ordered. 'Then let's hit the trail out of this flea-pit burg.'

The gambler told the gathering about how Baldwin had conned Rupe Lambert into waiting outside of town for him to come on the scene.

'Lambert thought that Baldwin was setting me up for him to take his revenge on me.'

Then Largo went on to relate how foxy Baldwin had been.

'He followed me out of town. Got the drop on me at the creek. Invited Rupe Lambert to join him, and then shot him in cold-blood, figuring to lay the blame on me. He planned to haul me back here to do what you fellas tried to do just now.'

Largo explained Baldwin's neck-tie scheme to incriminate him in Rupe Lambert's murder.

'Only that didn't quite work out the way he'd planned.'

'Why would Baldwin want to shoot Rupe Lambert?' one of the mob asked.

'To silence him, of course,' Largo said.

He went on to explain Ed Baldwin's fear of Charles Lambert's retribution.

'Baldwin was on to a hiding, or worse, if Rupe told his old man about his cringing.'

'Makes sense,' Largo's quizzer opined, and admitted honestly, 'I'd piss my pants as well!'

Spence Waterman, though in a fury of having his fun grabbed from him, did not offer a challenge to the gambler's version of events. There was another idea forming in his devious brain. One that just might make him a fat reward.

Largo pointed to where Andy White was sneakily mounting a horse outside the saloon.

'That gent gave you fellas a bum-steer.'

Elinora Langford's rifle cracked. The hotel clerk's saddle-horn spun in the air. It corkscrewed against White's forehead, giving off a dull echo of injured bone. He swayed in the saddle and pitched forward on to the hitch-rail. Then, out cold, he tumbled on to the boardwalk.

'I guess these good folk are free to leave,' Doc Lonergan said.

Gus Reilly, picking up on Spence Waterman's sudden muteness and suspecting treachery, kept his mouth shut. He was thinking deep thoughts which, if compared, would be found to be of a very similar nature to Waterman's.

The crowd drifted away, heads down, ashamed now of their attempt to hang an innocent man.

Striding off, nursing his mashed nose, Waterman promised, 'You're goin' to pay for this, Largo.'

The gambler laid his boot on Waterman's butt and pitched him forward.

'The next time there won't be a dozen men backing you, mister. It could prove mighty unhealthy for you, if you come looking for me,' he warned.

Waterman picked himself up, eyes burning with hatred.

'I have other plans for you gambler,' he snarled.

'If I see you again, I'll kill you,' Largo promised.

The gambler thanked Lonergan for his assistance, both the previous night when Rupe Lambert had thrown down his challenge, and also for his brave stand against the odds of minutes before.

Lonergan accepted Largo's thanks, but offered a warning.

'Watch for Waterman. He holds a grudge longer than most men.'

'Obliged, Doc,' the gambler said. 'Now, Elinora honey, I guess we'd best be making tracks before anyone else takes an exception to our presence.'

Lonergan waved them off.

'If you're ever back this way I'll be glad if you drop by,' he invited. 'That's if I'm still around, of course. A man of my years takes each day as it comes.'

'You'll make a hundred, Doc,' Largo opined. 'A kind heart keeps a man going, when the odds say he should be long gone.'

As Largo and Elinora Langford rode out, some of the men who had hoped for a hanging lounged about muttering, their faces dour; their thoughts given over to what view Charles Lambert would take of events.

Gus Reilly was in deep conversation with a few of them. Waterman, shunning Reilly and his cohorts, faded into the background and slipped quietly away to follow his own plan.

Reilly, not trusting Waterman, had decided to plough his own furrow. He was telling the men he was gabbing with about his plan to enrich them and himself. His gaze followed the departing Largo and Langford.

'I figure Charles Lambert will be very generous when we haul that duo before him, gents.'

The day had lost its earlier brightness. The sky was darkening under the stormheads seeping up from the south. Lightning was tearing great jagged holes in the swirling blackness. The storm was some way off yet, but coming on fast. It might veer off, its path changed by the pressures coming up from the furnace-hot floor of the desert country over which it travelled. Storms were fickle and unpredictable, and could change course suddenly to trap an unlucky traveller in their fury.

Largo welcomed the storm. He knew that, although they had left Spicer's

Crossing blemish-free, they were still in great danger from those who would see rich pickings in delivering them up to Charles Lambert on the strength of Andy White's cock-and-bull story. A storm would dull men's eagerness for pursuit.

The gambler reckoned that Waterman and Reilly would be the prime motivators who would dangle the prospect of quick riches. He had seen Reilly in a huddle with some men as they'd ridden out of town, while Waterman had slunk away like Judas.

He needed to put fast miles between them and Spicer's Crossing.

6

An hour later, the storm broke and pitched the afternoon into night. Lightning bounced off the trail: a secondary road that was full of danger, which Largo had chosen to hopefully throw any pursuers off the scent, and to give them time to put distance on their side.

It was dangerous country they were travelling through. Not only were the underfoot conditions treacherous due to the trail's lack of use, but it was bordered on both sides by high rock faces that acted as a trap for the storm's lightning, making their passage one of constant danger. The sheen of the lightning reflecting off the rock faces of the canyons, ravines and gullies they passed through, was as dazzling as noon sun reflected from a mirror. It added greatly to the ever-present hazards, by almost continuously unsighting them on a trail on which a single wrong hoof-fall could spill them to instant death.

Great jagged forks of lightning menaced their passage, following on from each other so fast that it seemed the lightning was one long, continuous flash. It was more deadly than a snakebite, and a whole lot quicker to kill. The deluge, too, battered them; the rain chilling them as their body temperatures dropped under the storm's onslaught.

The trail was a rising one, climbing steadily into mountains whose passages could become fast, raging torrents as the fury of the storm intensified. The deluge turned the rock faces to waterfalls, as the stony ground at their summits offered no haven to the downpour which spilled over to crash down on them, threatening to sweep them from their mounts. The rainwater, trapped between the rock faces, steadily built up. Negotiable, as yet, the narrow pass would not remain so for long. Water was beginning to funnel through, a stream that could easily turn to a fast-flowing flood. Enough water, and they would be swept away and battered against the walls of the pass.

So far they had been lucky, but all around them was the sound of rushing water as canyons, gullies and ravines filled up. The wind, driven by the storm's intensity, swirled along the trail carrying its own dangers in the debris it swept along with it. Dislodged stones dropping from on high, could open a man's skull, and the scraggy trees with little hold in the thin soil, wind-driven, could whiplash a traveller, or stake him through.

Largo had gambled. Telling himself that that was what gamblers did, was of little consolation to him now. He would not have taken the trail he was on had he thought the storm would change direction again, and with such rapidity. He had watched it move off, only to see it cut back to bite its own tail, and feed on its own fury. The mountain trail he had taken could be their undoing faster than any posse. He had gambled on being well advanced, if not down the other side of the mountain and into the vastness of the desert country, before any pursuers would realize they had been duped. But they had progressed at a snail's pace. Now they were slowly grinding to a halt.

Largo knew that his luck could not hold for ever. Some hands promised to deceive. He had been dealt such a hand, but at a woefully early stage in the game.

For the first time he saw fear in Elinora Langford's eyes. Men she could deal with, nature was something else, and it terrified her. Largo drew alongside her to offer his company.

'We'll be fine, Elinora honey,' he promised her.

He hoped it was a promise he could keep.

7

The six men led by Gus Reilly, who had decided to try and snare Largo and Elinora Langford and deliver them up to Charles Lambert in the hope of gaining a handsome reward, were wishing they had remained in town. But like Largo, they too had been deceived by the storm's fickleness, and were now at the tempest's furious core, as it had yet again changed direction. They had taken the regular trail out of town, figuring that Largo would want to make tracks as fast as he could. Reilly cursed. He should have reckoned on Largo having enough savvy to realize that Charles Lambert would be grateful and generous to those who handed over his son's killer, and as a result would have tried trickery.

Reilly did not believe for a second that Largo and Elinora Langford were murderers. It troubled him none. He would not lose any sleep over repeating Andy White's tall tale, and handing over innocent folk. He had had enough of hanging around Spicer's Crossing. He'd seen towns die before, and Spicer's Crossing was well beyond saving.

Now, storm-battered, Gus Reilly had cottoned on to Dan Largo's trickery. Or maybe lunacy? Because there was risk with a capital R in the trail the gambler had chosen, and which he was now about to follow him on. He had taken a trail that most sane men had abandoned a long time ago due to its treacherous nature, and with a woman along too, Elinora Langford, tough as old shoe leather as she was, would delay Largo's progress. The question was: by how much? Not much, he figured. Elinora Langford had a whole lot of grit. More than a lot of men he'd known.

Reilly looked to the mountain, dark and brooding under the storm, but most of its spite had been spent and the storm was swiftly moving on, sweeping down over the flat, sandy country, sucking up new force from the hot desert terrain.

Gus Reilly knew the trail that Dan Largo had embarked on. He had, on a few hairy occasions when the law had been dogging his tail, rode the treacherous mountain track. It was a trail that climbed to the rim of a canyon, before dropping steeply down, a passage exhausting to man and beast. When the top of the canyon was reached, the trail narrowed to one that was barely the width of a horse, which, in parts, crumbled dangerously. Many men, most of whom were desperate with the law on their tails, had taken the trail, and many of them had paid the price. Up there, high in the mountains, a man's good fortune only lasted a second at a time.

'I figure they're goners, Gus,' a man called Skip Hollins suggested to the men's leader, as his gaze searched the storm-tossed mountain trail snaking upwards above them. 'Those gullies and canyons will be flooded by now. In my time I seen men swept right off that mountain. I guess we'd best head back to town.'

'Didn't figure Largo to be *loco*,' another of the reward-chasers, a beefy-shouldered man by the name of Russ Barrow, said. 'Taking that devil's trail with a petticoat in tow.'

'Didn't have much choice, when you come to think of it,' Reilly said. 'We'd have got him for sure on this trail.'

'Guess that's the end of any reward,' Skip Hollins sighed.

'End of any reward?' Reilly snorted. 'I'm sure as hell not going to let go of my dream until I'm dead, or that damn gambler and the skirt are on Lambert's doorstep.' Grimly, he finished. 'Dead or alive!'

Hollins was astounded.

'You're going after him?' He looked in awe at the storm-swept mountain. 'Up there, Gus? In a damn storm?'

'That's where I'm going.' His greedy eyes swept the other men. 'Who's riding with me?'

Largo's pursuers divided down the middle. Russ Barrow and a man called Scrimpy Hanley — a nick-name earned for his penny-pinching ways — lined up with Gus Reilly. Skip Hollins and the other two men took the trail back to Spicer's Crossing.

'You boys ain't goin' to live to spend any reward,' Hollins opined. 'You fellas are ridin' into a hell's brew of trouble, I reckon.'

'We'll live to split the reward three ways,' Russ Barrow predicted. 'While you *hombres* will be fightin' mongrels for scraps.'

Their parting was acrimonious, insults flying.

'Hope one of them canyons sucks you in,' Hollins spat, spitefully.

Gus Reilly's fist lifted Hollins out of his saddle, while Russ Barrow blasted a gun out of another man's hand. With much grumbling and ill-will, the reward-chasers chose their trails.

Reilly again cursed. The explosion of Barrow's six-gun would travel a long way. All he could hope for was that the storm would suck it up and hide it in its own fury.

*　*　*

On the mountain the explosion of Russ Barrow's pistol was barely audible, but Largo's ears pricked. In the storm's rage, it was impossible to put a distance to the sound. It could be near or far-off; way down the trail, or right round the next twist on it. There was no way of telling. With Elinora visibly tiring from the gruelling trek he would have to hole up as soon as he found shelter — if he found shelter. That would hand their chasers an advantage. He reasoned that if they were prepared to risk the trail in the raging storm with all the dangers the mountain presented, they were very strongly motivated — to the point of risking their very lives in the pursuit of their goal.

Elinora and he were high up in the mountain, with most of the cascading water now behind them. The men starting up would be facing the threat of being literally swept off the mountain. A man's motivation had to be strong to face that threat. He reckoned these were the bounty hunters he had feared. Men hunting a prize were determined men, and therefore extremely dangerous too.

★   ★   ★

Spence Waterman had decided on a less risky scheme, which he hoped would be as profitable as the one Gus Reilly and the others had hared off on. The day before he had heard Rupe Lambert talk about his father having gone across the Rio to visit the Mex cathouse he had a fondness for. Word had it that he was a long-staying man when he got the urge, sometimes spending a week or more sampling the Mex whores, taking each one of the thirteen women in turn. That's where he was headed now. He had a hand in mind that, if played well, would, he figured, put him in good stead with Charles Lambert.

★ ★ ★

Dan Largo screwed up his eyes against the sheen of lightning and the grit and debris-laden wind of the narrow, twisting trail ahead. The trail had steadily decreased in width and condition, until now it was nothing more than a rutted track, where a mule would be hard-pushed to find purchase, let alone a horse.

He was faced with a dilemma. Tracks snaked off in different directions, some of which no doubt would wind back on the trail they had traversed, and which their pursuers would now be on. The last thing he needed was a nasty surprise, such as coming face to face, unprepared, with the hard cases determined to trade him and Elinora to Charles Lambert. He'd give as good as he got himself, but the harsh terrain and spiteful climate had tired Elinora Langford to the point of utter exhaustion, and she was in no fit condition to engage in a fight.

He drew rein and studied the trail ahead. One or more of these mule tracks would lead down the other side of the mountain. Some would wander without an end. While others would go nowhere except over the rim of a canyon. On a better day a man could leisurely explore his options, but in the teeth of a storm, with bounty hunters on their tails, Dan Largo had to make up his mind. Fast!

8

Gus Reilly, keeping the pot of gold that Charles Lambert would, he reckoned, hand over on deliverance of the man who had killed his son, gave dogged pursuit that was not normal in a man who preferred to lounge instead of toil; steal instead of earn.

Russ Barrow, losing his grit for the hellish trail, kept up a constant moan.

'You sure you've figured this right, Gus?'

Reilly glanced at the trail that looked like a black snake wriggling upwards and said, 'They're on this mountain for sure.'

'Maybe we should hole up,' Scrimpy Hanley suggested. ''Til the storm blows itself out.'

A light-framed man, he clung precariously to his mount, the wind more than once having threatened to sweep him from his saddle.

'Losing time ain't smart, Scrimpy,' was Gus Reilly's testy retort. 'Largo won't.'

Barrow said, 'He's got the woman. She'll be all tuckered-out by now. He'll have to rest up.'

'Having Elinora Langford along will slow him some, sure enough,' Reilly agreed. 'But she's a tough bird. She'll stay in the saddle for as long as she has to. That's what we've gotta do, too.'

Expression implacable, Gus Reilly faced in to the storm.

★　★　★

Spence Waterman had no such problems. He had the heat and uncertainty of the desert country to contend with, but he had left Spicer's Crossing with plenty of water and a spare horse, so his journey was one of reasonable comfort. The desert could throw up all sorts of surprises, natural and man-made. It was home to men who were suspicious of any stranger, and seldom took a chance of becoming acquainted, most times opting for safety by killing strangers, no questions asked. Nature, too, could be spiteful. The desert had a luring quality that, if not watched for, could have a man wandering until he dropped of exhaustion or went *loco*. Its predators were ever-watchful for, and suspicious of, intruders. The desert was littered with the bleached bones of fools.

And there was the Apache. Unpredictable and dangerous.

Though the dangers were many, Waterman reckoned that they were less than trying to nail Dan Largo and Elinora Langford, as Gus Reilly had decided to do. He was betting on information about Rupe Lambert's killing, and where his killers could be found, to hand him his reward from Charles Lambert.

In his opinion, Gus Reilly was a fool. Largo would probably kill him long before they reached the pass. But if he did not, the Apaches certainly would. Charles Lambert, with the army of men he could assemble, might stand a chance of surviving an Apache onslaught, but no one else would. Waterman took comfort in the knowledge that, if his plan came to fruition, he'd have his reward and be nowhere near danger when all hell broke lose.

There was only one fly in his ointment. Waterman hoped that when the time came to implement the most terrifying part of his preparations to convince Charles Lambert of his good faith, he would have the grit to go through with it.

He was making good progress. He knew the country, which was a big advantage. In his days as a gunfighter and outlaw, professions he had not been an outstanding success at, because he was not an intelligent man and took chances that other more successful exponents of those trades did not, he had during many a chase learned to survive in the lonely places and had acquired the skills and stamina to do so.

A lot of men, those who did not know or respect the desert country, found that their contempt for nature had often been their undoing.

Though, as yet, his passage had been trouble-free, he frequently dismounted and scanned the terrain around him for sign. The dreaded Apache, though not as great in number and well marshalled by the cavalry, still prowled their natural domain, acting up now and then to some offence the white man gave, particularly those entering or defiling their sacred places; places like the pass, where word had it Dan Largo and Elinora Langford were headed. Riding in there was the act of a fool, and not worth all the gold in the world, because a man wouldn't get to spend a nickel of any reward to be found in that terrible place.

* * *

As she swayed in the saddle, spent, Largo grabbed hold of Elinora Langford, coaxing, 'Stay on board for just a while longer, Elinora honey. We'll find shelter soon.'

How soon? And would it be soon enough?

9

The prospector's shack, cleverly set into a nest of boulders and using the rock face as its rear wall, was not up to much, but to Dan Largo right then it was a king's palace. He shook Elinora.

'Shelter.'

Her jaded green eyes took in the crumbling edifice, and she too saw a palace.

The positioning of the shack indicated that its builder had learned well from the fickleness of nature. The structure groaned and creaked and shifted as the storm curled over and around the sheltering boulders that formed the storm-defying cocoon. Refused entry, the gusting wind grew angrier, but the sheltered nook served its purpose and protected the shack from being uprooted and blown away.

It stunk of animals. There was a cot in the corner of the dark and unwelcoming shack, weaved from sapling branches, sagged by time and use. Largo sat Elinora on a rickety chair, whose seat had been weaved by the same expert hand. There was an askew-legged table littered with rotting food, a coal-oil lamp, some mining tools, a bunch of tallow candles, and a loop of fuse wire.

Largo carefully checked the bed for lice. He took it outside and upended it to shake loose any crawlers. Returning, he placed the weary Elinora on the cot. He lit the coal-oil lamp to relieve the premature dusk brought on by the storm. The lamp's bowl was only half-full. There was no more oil, so its glow would not last long. He placed the lamp on a chair near the cot and gave it a full wick to provide as much heat as it could to the shivering Elinora. Her face glowed with the fire of an impending fever, which he prayed would not become full-blown.

He went back outside to check Elinora's saddle-bags for any scraps.

Their hurried departure had not allowed time to stock up. His original plan had been to try his luck in Eagle Gap, a town only ten miles north of Spicer's Crossing, so he had not lumbered his horse with the extra weight of provisions.

There were hopeful streaks of blue in the milling clouds to the east, whose emergence was quickly swallowed up by the tumbling storm clouds. But their determined re-emergence gave Dan Largo a sense of hope that soon the storm would pass. Of course storms were notoriously fickle, driven as they were by the rapidly-changing air masses of the desert country. he'd been taken by surprise once already, and he had the feeling that before his jaunt to Skull Pass was completed, there would be many more surprises to contend with.

* * *

Russ Barrow was moaning again.

'Fightin' this storm don't make much

sense, Gus,' he told Reilly. 'If we ain't real careful, we'll be blowed right off this pile o' rock.'

If the swirling winds picked out Barrow for such a fate, Reilly would not shed any tears. A whinger in any group fighting the elements was the last thing that group needed. He should have known that having Barrow along would be more of a hindrance than a blessing, him being a natural moaner.

'You hear me, Gus?' he whined above the wind that seemed to fill every inch of the gully they were riding through with the wailing of lost souls.

'I hear ya, Russ,' Reilly called back, forcing a friendly tone, though he was feeling far from placatory towards Barrow. He glanced to a sky beginning to show fitful streaks of blue and orange, like pretty ribbons blowing in the darkness, and predicted, 'The storm's almost spent.'

'I dunno, Gus,' Barrow whinged. 'I seen blowers like this one hang 'round for quite a spell. Sometimes promising, only to fool ya in the long run.'

Scrimpy Hanley, as tired as Reilly was with Barrow's non-stop whining, snapped, his mouth a rattrap, 'Shush your damn gripin', Russ. Gus is right. The storm's vented its spleen.'

'Gus?' Barrow wailed, seeking Reilly's assurance that the storm was losing its spite.

'Like I told ya, Barrow,' he spat. 'The storm's more or less done for.'

Gus Reilly, a law-dodger for twenty years, had experienced the vagaries of nature from Alaska to the South Americas, where he'd spent time in Honduras riding with cattle-rustlers, staying out of the reach of a dogged US marshal who had tracked him into Mexico and had forced him to travel further to avoid his clutches.

Russ Barrow, not having the grit to buck both men's views, was left with no option but to agree with them. The only other option open to him was to make tracks back down the mountain, with all the dangers that such a trip would hold for a man who, in essence, was a town-man, being more at home in a saloon than toughing it out on the trail.

Resigned, he said, 'I guess you fellas know what you're spoutin' 'bout.'

Scrimpy Hanley closed the gap between himself and Reilly. When he drew level with Reilly, he said, 'I figure Barrow ain't goin' to be much use to us Gus, when lead starts flying. And I'm real tired of his bladderin'.'

'That, Scrimpy,' Gus Reilly agreed, 'is a view I share.'

They rode on together for a spell longer. Their conversation unfinished, each man left it up to the other to make the proposal that was on both their minds. Reilly finally made it.

'I reckon a two-way split of that reward would be sweeter than a three-way share-out, Scrimpy.'

Scrimpy Hanley smiled a surprisingly easy smile, not at all hinted at in his sharp features.

'Much sweeter, Gus,' he said.

Reilly fell back, allowing the hapless

Russ Barrow to catch him up. Barrow, not a natural horseman, and riding a horse prone to bouts of sourness, had struggled to master the animal every inch of the way up the mountain trail. The horse, a proud one, was contemptuous of its bungling rider, and acted up even more than it normally would have. Though at first annoyed by Barrow's lack of horse riding skill, Gus Reilly now saw it as a blessing for the plan that was fermenting in his mind.

'What were you and Hanley jawin' 'bout just now?' Barrow enquired suspiciously.

'About those lazy days ahead of us, when we collect Lambert's reward.'

Russ Barrow's eyes became greedy with dreaming.

'You figure Lambert will be generous, Gus?'

'The way I hear it, he's real generous to friends. And that's what we'll surely be once we deliver up the man who murdered his boy.'

Barrow's eyes clouded with worry.

'Thing is, Gus. Dan Largo and Elinora Langford didn't murder Rupe Lambert. We all heard Andy White say he was tall-taleing us.'

Gus Reilly guffawed and slapped Barrow on the back.

'But we sure ain't goin' to tell Lambert that, Russ.'

Barrow frowned.

'Truth be known, Gus. It don't settle none too easy with me. Tradin' a man's life for shekels.'

In that moment, Russ Barrow signed his death warrant.

10

Largo held his tobacco tin under the gushing water spilling off the shack's slanting roof and kept it there, overflowing, until the crust of grime inside the tin loosened and floated free. Not all of it, but then it would take a week, if not more, of rushing water to do that. He needed the tin to use as a frying pan to cook the few scraps of bacon he'd found in his saddle-bag. He had also dug up a couple of biscuits and some Java beans. It would be a meagre and miserable meal, but it was all there was to hand.

'It's all we've got,' Dan Largo said, handing Elinora Langford the sparrow offerings. 'The coffee will heat you some,' he encouraged her, as she showed little interest in partaking of the tarry brew.

Elinora sipped the coffee, her face

curling at its smoky acidity. She managed a weak smile. 'I've tasted better.'

The gambler, looking into Elinora Langford's wan face, saw the woman behind the mask she showed to the world; the softer, beguiling woman that she hid away so well. Her accent held a trace of the South. Tennessee maybe? He said as much.

Her flushed face, and the diamond-bright perspiration on her forehead, worried him. Fever, as Largo knew — having suffered several bouts as an odd-jobbing travelling man, before he had the sense to seek a mentor in Dodge City to teach him the skills of card-playing — could jump either way.

Largo's mind went back to the shot he'd heard a couple of hours earlier. There had been nothing since, but that probably meant that if they had pursuers, they had learned from that mistake and had made stealthy progress since.

'Tennessee, indeed,' Elinora Langford murmured.

Her green eyes clouded with warm remembrance.

'The war?' Largo asked, guessing her train of thought.

She nodded.

'It took everything. Father and two brothers. Mother died six months later of a broken heart. Greenglades, my home, was looted and burned by Yankee soldiers.'

Tears filled her eyes. Through her tears shone the horror of past events.

'It wasn't only property they took, Dan.'

Largo drew her into his arms. He'd been a Yankee soldier, and knew the awful crimes that were committed in the last dreadful weeks of the Civil War, as the South crumbled in chaos, and normally law-abiding men, filled with festering hate and unaccustomed power, became the kind of men who'd live out the rest of their lives under a shadow of shame because of the deeds they had done.

Largo could still see the burning

homes. Hear the screams of violated women. See the hanging trees where men who had worn the rebel grey swung in the breeze. The scorched fields and burning towns. Scenes whose violence and cruelty had burned a hole in his brain.

It had taken a long time to cleanse his dreams of the images of carnage and pillage that inevitably is the lot of the vanquished. Even now, several years on and myriad trails later, Dan Largo still had his restless nights.

Largo cradled Elinora in his arms, letting her choose her own time to speak. It took a long time for the horrors in her mind to be chased back in to the darkness. The storm had drifted away. The clatter of rain on the shack's roof had settled to a whisper. The furious wind had become a breeze.

Elinora Langford told her story.

'When the war was near lost,' she sighed, 'my father, who had travelled extensively in Africa and traded in diamonds and precious stones, dispatched my Uncle Willie, who had weak lungs and was not fit to bear arms, to London with a pouch of diamonds and precious stones.

'Daddy figured that a subjugated South would not be worth living in. The family would need assets abroad to live on until the South reasserted its independence, which he was certain it would, and we could return.'

Elinora smiled ruefully.

'He reckoned the Union would come to its senses, and sooner or later adopt the policies which had started the conflict.'

Troubled, Largo asked, 'Your father owned slaves?'

It troubled him more when, with pride, Elinora Langford declared, 'Fifty or more.'

'I never did agree with one man owning another,' the gambler said dourly.

'Has the black man done any better after the war?' she challenged him.

He had to admit, 'No. He hasn't.'

'I know the negro hadn't much dignity in the South,' Elinora said defiantly, 'and there was wrong-doing that needed to be addressed. But I reckon the black man isn't any better off in the shiny new Union.'

Dan Largo found himself without a countering argument, having witnessed the prejudiced and often malicious treatment of the former slaves.

Elinora took his hands in hers.

'Let's not go over old ground, Dan,' she said softly. 'I'd much prefer to look to the future.'

He smiled. 'I can't argue with that.'

He teased her lips with his. Her kiss was as sweet as honey and as warm as a summer breeze. When it was over, Dan Largo knew that, finally, he had been snared by a woman. It surprised him even more to find that he liked the idea.

Elinora continued the tale of her family's misfortune.

'Daddy had not chosen well. Uncle Willie, through no fault of his own, was not a fitting messenger to entrust so much to. He went down a hundred and one side-tracks, most of which made no sense then or now, en route to England. I guess in war there are no straight lines. Somehow, Willie found himself in Skull Pass with the diamonds.'

Revealed at last, the reason behind her passionate desire to reach the Indian sacred place.

'There, he and the slaves with him, found themselves at the mercy of the Apache, of which there was none shown,' she said bitterly.

'Like I told you,' the gambler said. 'The white man going anywhere near that place is bad medicine, Elinora.'

'By some miracle, Joshua, Father's personal slave whom he'd sent with Uncle Willie, got himself out of there, and finally found me in Denver where I was dealing blackjack in a saloon.'

Largo's eyebrows arched.

'I did a whole lot worse to survive after the war, Dan. It's best you know that now. So that you can get it out of the way or make it a barrier.'

'I'm not criticizing,' the gambler drawled. 'I'm not exactly lily-white myself.'

She continued: 'Joshua brought me a letter, entrusted to him by Uncle Willie, for delivery to any surviving member of the family. I was the only one left.'

'Joshua risked life and limb through Indian country and over the trails to find you with the letter?' Largo asked incredulously.

'Of course,' Elinora answered matter-of-factly, not understanding Largo's bemusement. 'Joshua was given a task to complete and he did just that.' Her eyes dropped. 'Sadly, after doing so he was run down by a drunk in charge of a buckboard minutes later.'

Again, matter-of-factly, she informed Largo. 'I shot the drunken no-good.'

'They let you ride out of Denver after killing this drunk?' Largo enquired.

Elinora laughed. 'Let's just say that the Mayor didn't want his wife to know about his . . . shall we say . . . prefer-ences.'

She plunged her hand down between her breasts to retrieve a yellowed parchment. She handed the letter to Largo, then pulled it back a little as he reached for it.

'I'm trusting you like I haven't trusted a man in a long time, Dan,' she said. 'I sincerely hope that my trust is not misplaced.'

'It isn't,' he assured her. Then smilingly asked, 'And if it was?'

Chillingly, Elinora Langford replied, 'I'd kill you.'

Holding her gaze with his, Dan Largo said, 'I believe you would at that, Elinora.'

My, oh my, he thought. What a woman! He read Uncle Willie's letter. It began:

To the Langford or Langfords who will survive the war.

And went on:

I have done my best to complete the task set me, but I have failed. My mistakes have been many, and have led me to this hellish place whose real name I do not know, but which I shall call Skull Pass. Our guide was bitten by a snake and died. The Apache are massing. We all face death.

I hope that Joshua, that most loyal of servants, will escape this hostile and ungodly place to deliver my letter to you. I am enclosing a map of this wretched place, which the guide drew for me before he died.

It is sunset.

The last line of Uncle Willie's letter read:

The cache of diamonds will be found at the tip of the Vulture's Beak.
                              Uncle Willie.

The gambler handed the letter back to Elinora. 'Makes for interesting reading.'

'What does the last line mean, Dan?'

Largo had no answer.

'I guess we'll see what Uncle Willie meant when we get there,' she sighed.

'Riding into Skull Pass is like riding into hell,' Largo cautioned. 'It's the kind of heat that boils a man's brain, Elinora.'

'You think Uncle Willie went crazy?'

'I'm saying that it should be considered. Did Joshua know of this vulture that your uncle talks about?'

'We didn't have time to talk. I was dealing black-jack when he put in an appearance. He gave me the letter. We were to meet later. The drunken buckboard driver put paid to that.'

'A tough break,' Largo sympathized. 'Are you still bent on going to that hell-hole, on the word of a man who was probably out of his head with fear and heat?'

'I am.'

'You rest now, Elinora,' he said kindly. 'Dream your dreams about those diamonds.'

For a moment, a stark fear showed in

her eyes. He understood well what that fear was and reassured her.

'I'll be right here when you wake up.'

She hugged him.

'Sorry I doubted you, Dan.'

'Don't be. Doubt is a fine and healthy thing in a woman who's just met a strange man.'

Elinora laughed.

'I experienced the full range of your strange ways last night, Dan Largo,' she teased. 'And I'm not complaining.'

He laughed along with her.

When she settled down, Largo said, 'I reckon I'll fill my lungs before turning in.'

The storm had now passed and the encroaching night was balmy and smelled of fresh rain; a freshness that would only last until shortly after sun-up. He strolled casually to the door of the shack, resisting the urge in his legs to hurry.

Seconds earlier he had heard the clatter of a sliding stone, abruptly curtailed. Something or someone had stopped its slide.

He was betting on it being *someone*.

11

Riding alongside Russ Barrow, Gus Reilly hogged the inside track. Barrow worriedly looked ahead to where the narrow trail skirted a ravine.

Reilly edged closer to Barrow.

'Pretty shitty trail, huh, Gus?' Barrow said conversationally, as if he were casually discussing the difficult terrain with a compatriot of equal riding skills, rather than giving Reilly a hint that there would not be room up ahead for them to ride safely together.

'I've ridden worse, Russ,' Reilly drawled. 'Of course you're a town man.' He laughed mockingly. 'Used to orderly traffic and straight roads.'

'I ain't always been a town johnnie,' Barrow flung back, piqued by Reilly's scoffing tone.

'Yeah?' The scoff in Gus Reilly's tone deepened.

'Yeah!' Barrow glowered, and boasted, 'I was on a cattle drive once.'

Reilly snorted derisively.

'A cattle drive, huh? A nice ambling pace over flat plains on well-traversed trails, I guess.'

To Gus Reilly, used to riling men until their pride overcame their good sense, Russ Barrow was easy meat. The plan he had hatched since talking earlier with Scrimpy Hanley was about to be enacted.

'There were rough times on that drive, too!' Barrow argued hotly.

'I bet,' Reilly sneered. 'Like that awful day the beans ran out!'

The ravine loomed. Reilly smiled secretly on seeing the jagged rocks that littered its floor, many as pointed as a dagger. His sneer took on a new depth of mocking.

Incensed by Reilly's jibes, Russ Barrow had completely forgotten the approaching danger, and had totally given over his concentration to restoring his pride.

Gus Reilly took satisfaction in having achieved his goal. Barrow felt himself jostled. It was too late to do anything about his topple off the trail into the ravine. His last sight was of Gus Reilly's gloating face. The last sound he heard was his own cry following him down into the abyss.

From then on, Reilly was careful to leave a gap between him and Scrimpy Hanley. Just in case Hanley would get the idea that the entire reward was better than a two-way split, seeing that getting rid of Russ Barrow had been his idea first.

⋆　⋆　⋆

Opening the shack door, Dan Largo was careful to maintain an air of calm casualness. Not wanting to alert any would-be watchers to the fact that he was aware of their presence, he rolled a smoke with the air of a man without troubles, searched his pockets for a lucifer and cursed. Just like a man inconvenienced, he returned back inside the shack and brought back with him the coal-oil lamp to light his smoke, with not the slightest hint in his gait of having used its yellow light to peruse the terrain immediately in the vicinity of the shack.

He had seen nothing. But he had heard the rustle of undergrowth as the lamp-light, tossed by the breeze, suddenly and unexpectedly extended its light in a long, narrow shaft to the right of the shack and a clutch of spindly trees of mixed origins, trying to survive in the shale among a tumble of boulders.

It was good cover.

Soon it would be dark.

As Largo returned inside the shack, he was in a contemplative mood. Should he take action now, while it was still twilight? Or should he wait for dark? His gambler's instincts taking over, he carefully weighed the odds favouring his options.

Whatever his choice, it was a bind he'd prefer not to be in.

12

Spence Waterman had made dogged progress. At the time Dan Largo was assessing his odds, he was within sight of the exclusive Mex cathouse, standing in the middle of nowhere just the other side of the Rio Grande, where men who didn't want to catch the pox that ordinary whores might be carrying, took their pleasures at a price that most men's pockets could not stretch to.

He had arrived at Charles Lambert's favourite den of iniquity.

The pleasure house was owned and run by a Parisian woman called Babette Dumas. Her kin, having fled to the Americas just before the rest of their kind lost their heads to the revolutionary blade, had settled in New Orleans. The family's fortunes had suffered many setbacks until, when Babette arrived on the scene thirty years previously, her mother had started — what had become for Babette Dumas — the family business.

Waterman, pleased on the one hand that he'd made swift progress, had his pleasure stunted by what he now had to do. Just riding in to cut short Charles Lambert's pleasures with a tall tale, without evidence of its veracity, could bring the wrong reaction. Spence Waterman had heard too many bone-chilling stories about Lambert's fiery responses to what he figured to be lies.

Gritting his teeth, Waterman slid his pistol from its holster, laid its barrel at an angle to his left side just below his ribs in the softer flesh of his belly, and hoped that he'd get his next act right. He steadied the tremble in his hand, but did not bother to wipe the sweat from his brow. In the next couple of seconds he'd be awash in sweat.

If the next second or two went awry, all the money in the world would not matter to him.

★ ★ ★

Back in the mountains, some thirty
miles east of where Spence Waterman
was trying to keep control over his
rumbling gut, Gus Reilly and Scrimpy
Hanley were crouched near the shack
where Dan Largo and Elinora Langford
had taken refuge from the storm, trying
to gauge the fickle flame of the lamp
that the gambler was holding to light
his quirly with. Only seconds before,
the lamp's sudden flare had almost
revealed Hanley. They wondered if
Largo had picked up on the slight rustle
of undergrowth as he readjusted his
position? It didn't seem so. He was
returning inside the shack, seemingly
unconcerned.

★ ★ ★

Back inside the shack, Dan Largo's
mind was racing. Having calculated the
odds, he had reached the conclusion
that a direct assault on the watchers

outside would be fraught with all sorts of dangers, all of them deadly. How many lurkers were there? Where were they? The bushes to the right of the shack had rustled as the lamp-light skirted them, but maybe that was just some night creature frightened by the lamp's glow? Maybe there was no one out there at all? Maybe his nerves were acting up? But he'd have to reckon on having company of the two-legged kind.

They had the advantage too of having eyes used to the dark, whereas his would take precious seconds to reach their level of awareness, once he was outside the shack. The lamp-light was not a powerful light, leaving great swathes of shadow in the small shack, but it was still light that his eyes had become familiar with and had adjusted to.

He could wait for them to make a move, but that would rob him of the element of surprise. And what if they simply decided to torch the shack? There was plenty of scrub in the terrain around the shack to make burning it an easy task. But it was wet scrub. How easy would it be to ignite it? If he was forced into the open, he'd face their waiting guns.

That would make him a dead man!

Of course, if they were the bounty hunters that Largo reckoned they were, it would be preferable to take them alive and parade them in front of Charles Lambert, allowing him to deliver his own particular brand of justice. The gambler figured that with a man like Lambert, who lived by his own laws and handed out his own brand of justice, it would be a case of the more pleasure given, the greater the reward bestowed.

On the other hand, the reward-chasers might figure that dead evidence was every bit as good as the live kind.

Largo was quickly reaching the conclusion that whatever way he played the cards handed him, he'd need the devil's own luck to come out of it with his and Elinora Langford's skin intact.

He had to pick an option and go with it. Sitting around second-guessing the intentions of their pursuers was the worst option of all.

He'd been lucky as a gambler. However, he knew that every winning streak finally ran out.

'Dan . . . ' Largo looked to Elinora sitting on the edge of the cot. Lost in his own thoughts, he had not noticed her watching him. 'What is it?'

'Oh just daydreaming.'

She came to stand alongside him. When she spoke, her voice was soft and caring.

'For a gambler, you're a God-awful liar, Dan Largo.'

Cornered, Largo had no choice but to outline their predicament, and was about to go with Elinora's option of shooting it out, with all the terrible risks that that entailed, when his eye came to rest on a possible solution to their problem.

It was a bluff to beat all bluffs. But, hell, he was a gambler. His ruse, with a dollop of luck and some mighty fine acting, might just work.

13

Across the desert another man was about to take a gamble which, if it backfired, could prove to be every bit as fatal as Dan Largo's dice with chance. Spence Waterman gritted his teeth and pulled the Colt's trigger. The burn of the .45's bullet seared through the soft flesh of his belly, and the pain staggered him dangerously. His heart thundered in his chest, bouncing about like a cork on choppy water. For a second he thought his luck had gone bad, and the bullet had sunk through his gut, rather than just grazing it as intended. As the terrible seconds of uncertainty passed and he was still standing, the joy of taking the gamble that was necessary if he was to convince Charles Lambert that he'd tried his best to help his son Rupe, acted as a balm for his pain. Riding across the desert, he had feared that when the time came to put the finishing touch to his deception, being a cowardly man when it came to pain, he might not have had the nerve to do what he'd just done.

Head spinning, as shock set in to shake his body from head to toe, Waterman forced his pain aside. He went down and grabbed a handful of the sandy, brown soil, and caked it on the wound to blacken and age it. Rubbing the earth into the open wound was a risky business. Infection would surely set in. He consoled himself with the thought that an angry wound, got in defence of his son, would probably make Charles Lambert even more appreciative when it came to handing out a reward.

Task completed, he lay back against a tree-trunk in the hollow he planned to spend the night in, hoping that his timing was not off, and by morning infection would not have progressed to weaken him too much. It worried him that the wound continued to bleed, and he waited anxiously for coagulation to begin.

He slept fitfully. He had been shot several times in varying degrees of severity, and knew the feel of a gunshot wound going bad. Infection was setting in faster than he'd anticipated. Deep in the night, Spence Waterman began to fret that his scheme to wring dollars from Charles Lambert by a liar's tale of murder, was going to be his final scam in a life of lies and treachery.

★ ★ ★

Elinora Langford listened to Dan Largo's plan with growing astonishment and concluded, 'It'll never work, Dan!'

'Do you have a better idea?' he asked somewhat testily.

She realized that her quick-fire rejection of his scheme had been too starchy.

'No. Sorry.'

'Then . . . ' Largo held up the bunch

147

of tallow candles in his hand, 'this is all we've got.'

He cut a section from the loop of fuse wire left behind by the prospector whose shack they had taken over, and tied it into the bunch of candles, purposely letting a short fuse show to add urgency to anyone seeing it loop through the air towards them. This would make it necessary for them to move quickly, and by so doing reveal themselves, hopefully handing the advantage to him. He scrutinized the candles to see if they could pass for dynamite. His confidence was not high.

Starting for the door, he said, 'Wish me luck, Elinora honey.'

She came to him and held him fiercely.

'You've come to mean a whole lot to me, Dan.'

Largo had never counted on being boosted by a woman's gentle words, but he was now. His lips found hers, he hoped, not for the last time.

'Remember. We've got to be ace

actors to pull this off.' He drew her with him to the door, and lit the fuse. 'Ready?'

She held up crossed fingers.

'Ready.'

Largo yanked open the door, stepped outside, threw the buckshee dynamite charge, and yelled, 'Duck!'

He grabbed Elinora around the waist and dived back inside the shack. He was a whole lot happier when a man excitedly hollered, 'Shit! Dynamite!'

Peacemaker spitting, Largo sprinted to the side of the shack. Scrimpy Hanley, eyes agog with fright, was leaping from cover to seek a new safe haven.

'Ain't so,' Gus Reilly shouted to his partner, but too late.

Dan Largo's Peacemaker kicked. Scrimpy Hanley was spun in the air and smashed against a boulder. His cocked gun exploded in his face and blasted off the roof of his head.

Gus Reilly, a veteran of such skirmishes and therefore a fast thinker, recognized Largo's sleight of hand for what it was. If he had real dynamite he'd have used it long before now, and not with the theatrical embellishment he'd engage in, designed to scare. Well, he'd scared Scrimpy Hanley sure enough.

Reilly waited. He was not a rushing kind of man. Caution had kept him alive for nigh on twenty years of hell-raising, and he valued its contribution to his survival. He'd circle close, keeping out of range from any gun the woman might be packing. He had seen her split the hanging rope around Largo's neck with a single shot, and was not of a mind to offer himself as a target to her.

It would take time to get close to Largo, but he had time. Better to be patient with time, than end up with no time at all.

Sinking into the shadows at the side of the shack that was blind to Gus Reilly, Dan Largo knew that his crude trick had only been partly successful.

There was at least one more, and maybe a lot more. But he was counting on one only, reasoning that if the man he'd downed had more than one partner they would have been spread out and, as the buckshee dynamite was only going in one direction, they would not have been under threat and would have opened up on him.

The problem now was how to flush the other man from cover. To do so, he would have to take another and even greater risk. He would have to tempt him beyond his ability to resist.

If only she had a gun! Elinora Langford cursed her misfortune in having left her rifle in its saddle scabbard. Dan's opponent was a patient man and therefore a dangerous one. He could have tried for Largo as he sought the cover of the side of the shack, but he'd resisted the urge to nail Dan that had to be burning a hole in his gut.

Fear and longing for Dan had punched a great yawning hole in her heart. If he were killed now, Elinora

Langford knew that, should her life span a hundred years, it would not close again. She loved Dan Largo; loved him too much for even the riches waiting in Skull Pass to make any difference now.

She stepped out of the shack, and strode purposefully to where her horse was hitched.

It was a night of surprises for Gus Reilly. He had seen a rifle in the woman's saddle scabbard, and it looked like she was headed straight for it. She was *loco*. She had to be!

'Hold it right there, lady,' Reilly ordered Elinora from the darkness.

Elinora ignored his order and kept on walking. The more he spoke, the greater Largo's chance of pinning down his location.

'I'll damn-well drop you,' Reilly warned.

Elinora Langford kept on walking.

Largo had hoped to pick his own time to implement the next phase of his plan to lure the lurker out, but Elinora's *loco* antics left him with no time at all!

A bullet bit the ground in front of her, and his heart tumbled.

Largo sprang from cover, gun blasting in the direction of Gus Reilly's voice, while knowing that in the mountains and the night, he could be shooting in entirely the wrong direction. His hope was that by offering himself as a target, his plan to tempt his opponent to risk showing himself to finish him off would work.

It did.

Reilly reared up from the scrub like a hellish demon, rifle tracking Largo as he dashed to protect Elinora. The Winchester spat. Largo felt a burn on his left shoulder, thankful for the rock that he'd tripped over. In his stumble, he pulled Elinora to the ground with him. He pushed her behind a boulder and snapped an order.

'Stay there!'

Then he corkscrewed up, Peacemaker blasting.

When Largo stumbled, Gus Reilly

knew that good fortune favoured the gambler. This opinion was proven correct when, a second later, Reilly felt a mighty thud in his chest, and his innards were ripped apart. The last thing he felt was the gut-wrenching tug on his back as the Peacemaker's load blasted through, leaving a ragged hole.

Worried by what might have happened to the woman he was now certain he was in love with, Largo reacted angrily.

'What in hell were you playing at, Elinora?'

'I was trying to lure him out by offering myself as a target,' she explained, shrinking from Largo's anger. Then reacting to his fiery rebuke, declared hotly, 'And my plan worked, damn you!'

A moment later their anger was lost in each other's arms.

'Offering yourself as a target was a crazy thing to do, Elinora,' he gently scolded.

'I guess bucking the odds is something that rubs off on a gal when she's in love with a gambler,' Elinora murmured. 'Besides, you didn't seem to have an idea in your head to flush that no-good out.'

He smiled. 'Brains and beauty in one package. Aren't I the lucky fella, Elinora Langford?'

'How were you going to flush him out anyway?' she enquired, as they went back inside the shack.

'Like you said, Elinora honey. I hadn't an idea in my head.'

'And what's so darn funny?' she asked, as a slow smile spread across Dan Largo's lips.

14

Charles Lambert stood buck naked in front of Spence Waterman, still showing the signs of only seconds before having left the whore whom he was in bed with, the third that night. Waterman had heard stories about Lambert's physical dimensions, and had, like most who had heard the same stories, laughed. But it was no laughing matter — the evidence to back up those stories was right there in front of him and, frankly, the stories had erred on the conservative side.

'What's this about Rupe?' Lambert barked, angry at having had his pleasures interrupted, and clearly anxious to resume his tryst with the woman on his arm. 'You go and powder your ass honey,' he growled at the fawning woman.

The woman threw Waterman a

spiteful glare and pouted out of the cathouse's plushly-carpeted and elegantly-furnished sitting-room.

Babette Dumas, the cathouse madam, had taken a whole lot of persuading to interrupt Lambert's jousting. Still nervous, she fidgeted with the cord of her black silk dressing gown. Once, a drunken client had wandered into Lambert's room. Piqued by the drunk's interruption of his pleasures, Lambert had slit his throat.

He was a brutish giant of man; the kind of man, folk would say, who had been needed to build the West, and also the kind of man who, now that the West was entering tamed times, was unable to change. He had come West in a wagon train, dirt-poor. He had fought Indians, matching them and some would say surpassing them in sheer cruelty and brutality. Anyone else who needed fighting, he'd fought and vanquished, too.

He had worked like a slave to build his first spread and ramrod his first cattle drive. After that he had shrewdly invested in railroads and banks. He had become a mortgage lender and showed no mercy with defaulters, grabbing their land to add to his own, and in truth never showing any qualms in grabbing what he wanted.

Like many great fortunes, Charles Lambert's wealth was made up of a little good luck and a whole lot of larceny.

Anyone who crossed paths with him and knew Rupe Lambert, were hard-pushed to figure out how such a man could have the kind of milk and water offspring that Rupe Lambert had been.

'You lost your tongue?' he glowered at Waterman, sending his Adam's apple bobbing.

'No-no, sir,' he stammered, feeling a constriction of his throat as if a giant's hand had encircled it.

'Well then,' Lambert growled.

'Y-yes, s-s-sir.'

'Some imp dancing on your tongue to make you talk like a fool, mister?' Lambert snarled. 'What about Rupe?'

At that moment, Spence Waterman wished he'd yielded to the urge to turn back that had assailed him as he had ridden up to the whorehouse. His life was a miserable one, true enough, but he was sucking air and things might always get better. However, if Lambert took a notion, and it did not take much to give him such notions, he'd kill him right on the spot.

'R-Rupe's dead, Mr Lambert,' he finally blurted out.

'Dead?' Lambert's voice was barely a whisper. The ruddiness of his face turned a slate-grey.

'Yes, sir. Fella by the name of Dan Largo, a no-good card-slick, done for him over in Spicer's Crossing. Rupe challenged the gambler when he had a run of luck that lasted longer than any run of luck should rightly have. Done for the sheriff too, Mr Lambert, sir, and this Largo's got a woman in tow, every bit as guilty.'

'A woman?' Lambert quizzed, regaining his composure. 'What woman?'

'A slut by the name of Elinora Langford.'

'Elinora Langford?' Lambert asked. 'What does this *slut* look like?'

Waterman obliged with a description of Elinora Langford, and wondered about Charles Lambert's total, but strange, interest in her.

'Blackjack dealer?' Lambert asked.

Waterman shrugged. 'I ain't heard, Mr Lambert. But it wouldn't surprise me none. She knows her way 'round a saloon.'

Lambert's gaze became distant. He was back on board the *Orleans Lady*, plying the Mississippi three years previously. Elinora Langford was dealing blackjack. He had accumulated sizeable winnings, every cent of which he had offered Elinora Langford, if she would join him in bed. She had refused, making it clear that being a blackjack dealer and being a whore did not necessarily go hand in hand, and particularly in her case.

Like most men, he held the belief

that a lady's *no* really meant *yes*. And on that premise had later gone to her room to find out that in Elinora Langford's case, *no* meant exactly that. She had backed up her stance with a slap to the face and a Derringer in his belly, which she used to back him out of her room and on to the deck in full view of an awe-struck audience.

His first instinct was for retribution and revenge. However, as the night wore on, his anger subsided, and in its place a strong admiration for Elinora Langford's courage took over. The next morning he had sought her out, only to find that she had left the *Orleans Lady* when the boat had berthed during the night to take on fuel.

Elinora Langford was the only woman, or man, who had had the gall to defy him, and that made her the woman he wanted to marry that morning. But he'd kill her now, if she had anything to do with his son's death.

'I was real lucky,' Waterman was displaying his self-inflicted wound. 'I

got this tryin' to stop Largo's murderous attack on Rupe.'

'Trying?' Lambert glowered. 'Seems
to me, with Rupe dead, you didn't try
hard enough, mister.'

Waterman's innards creaked. It looked
like Lambert was steaming towards
rage.

'You're absolutely sure that the
woman helped murder Rupe?'

Instinct told Waterman that he would
not want to hear that she had.

'Well, sir — '

'You said she did. Did she or didn't
she, dammit!'

Waterman's legs weakened under
Lambert's hellish glare. 'She's travellin'
with the gambler,' he said limply.

Lambert's rage eased. Waterman's
relief sharpened.

'I know where the devil's duo are
headed, Mr Lambert.'

'Where?' Lambert enquired sourly.

'The story 'round Spicer's Crossing
is that they're headed for some place
called Skull Pass.'

'Skull Pass?' Lambert asked, puzzled. 'I know every inch of the country, but — '

Waterman quickly explained. 'I reckon that Skull Pass ain't its right name though.'

Charles Lambert's anger was hotter than volcano lava.

'Don't talk in riddles, mister!'

Waterman cringed under Lambert's glare.

'I figure they're headed to that pass near the Mex border. The one that the Apaches get all het-up 'bout if a white man sets foot in it. They figure it spooks their spirits.'

Recognition of the pass that Waterman spoke of brought a look of stark disbelief to Lambert's face. He was well acquainted with its bloody history.

'You sure Rupe didn't put a hole in this Largo fella's head? No one with any marbles rides into that pass.'

Waterman shrugged and conceded.

'Don't make much sense. All I know is that Elinora Langford offered this fella Largo a pile of dollars to take her there.'

'Then that's where we're headed!' Lambert declared.

'Ah,' Waterman fretted. 'We?' His voice shook as if an earthquake had begun right under his feet.

Charles Lambert glared at him. 'You want to even the score with this Largo, don't you?'

'Well . . . '

Lambert's tone dropped to a chilling timbre. 'Square things for Rupe?'

Panic gripped Waterman. His plan for a quick reward and life in the South Americas was going badly awry. He filled his face with pain.

'Sure I do, Mr Lambert, sir. But I ain't a well man. This wound hurts somethin' awful. I reckon it's infected real bad.'

'Babette,' Lambert hollered. The whorehouse madam appeared as if by magic, filled with trepidation. 'Get the Apache woman.'

Babette Dumas vanished as fast as

she had appeared.

' 'Pache woman?' Waterman enquired, shakily.

'She can work magic with her potions. She'll have that wound cleaned, and you ready to ride in no time at all.'

He strode out of the room.

'Meanwhile, I'll round up a crew from the village a couple of miles south of here. We'll ride at first light.'

Waterman, his panic reaching new heights, found false bravery.

'Fact is, I was plannin' on restin' up here, and — '

'And?' Lambert interjected.

'Well, sir. I figured that my pain and the information I g-g-gave you . . . Well . . . '

'Are worth a reward?' Lambert snorted.

Waterman tried to confirm that view, but all that came from his mouth was a rasping croak that sounded like ripping calico.

'You'll get your reward,' Lambert

stated, 'when Largo pays the full price for my son's murder. And when you play your full part in delivering that payment.'

He came face to face with Waterman, and the no-good's heart skittered under Lambert's terrible scrutiny.

'Not a cent before then!'

The Apache woman came in carrying an earthen bowl of steaming foulness. Waterman blanched. As Lambert rode away from the whorehouse to search for the kind of cut-throats the nearby village could provide him with, Spence Waterman's screams filled the night.

15

Dan Largo placed the last stone on the twin graves of Gus Reilly and Scrimpy Hanley.

'You know any prayers?' he enquired of Elinora.

'Prayers? They didn't even deserve burying, Dan,' she said angrily. 'All we've done is waste time doing it.'

'I know they weren't worth much as men, Elinora,' Largo conceded, 'but it wouldn't be proper nor fitting to leave them here for wild animals to feed on.'

'How long do you think it'll take for them to get under those stones?' Elinora challenged.

'Not long at that, I reckon. But I'll rest easy knowing that I did the best I could.' He took her hands in his. 'And so will you, once that furnace temper of yours cools down.'

'Oh, Dan,' she said, leaning against

him. 'I just want us out of here. Right out of this country to Paris, France or London, England. Civilized living is what I hanker for. I've had enough of lawlessness and cruelty.'

Largo, though reluctant to do so, raised a possibility that had been nagging him since he had found out what was so important about Skull Pass.

'What if someone's already found the diamonds, Elinora?'

She paled.

'It's possible.'

'No, it isn't.'

Her hands fluttered at her red hair. 'It couldn't be, Dan. Say it couldn't be, damn it!'

He held her tightly. 'It might also turn out that Uncle Willie was hallucinating.' He held her tighter still as he felt her sag against him. 'All I'm asking is, what then?'

'I don't know, Dan,' she answered honestly. 'I've been dreaming for so long it might be hard for me to wake up to reality.'

Largo sighed heavily.

'Well, I guess we'd best go and find out if Uncle Willie was *loco* or not.'

The trail ahead, no great shakes to begin with, was brittle and uncertain underfoot after the storm, sometimes barely wide enough for a horse to pass. There were many hairy moments for Dan Largo and Elinora Langford, as they negotiated the narrow track round the rim of a canyon that meant certain death if a mistake was made, before being able to start down the mountain.

Many trees with roots set in sparse topsoil had been dislodged by the deluge, forcing the intrepid duo into precarious detours through rocks that had not yet resettled following the torrents which had swept over them, and which could slide from under a rider without warning. Other trees, desperately clinging to weakened roots, could, at any second, topple with devastating effect.

If their luck held, and they reached the desert country below, Indians would be only one threat they would have to contend with, and not always, in Largo's experience, the biggest threat. That could come from the many hard cases, no-goods and outlaws for whom the desert country was a safe refuge, most lawmen being reluctant to traverse its torturous terrain. And there were nature's predators, too.

But Largo worried more about Elinora Langford. Such a fine woman would be a mighty temptation to resist. Men, both red and white, would have her in their sights from the second she rode into the desert.

He really did not care a fig about the treasure in Skull Pass, Dan Largo already had all the treasure he needed in the woman riding companionably alongside him.

⋆　⋆　⋆

Spence Waterman had to admit that the foul-smelling balm which the Apache woman had liberally spread over his self-inflicted wound had taken the sting from it, and had replaced it with a warm comfort that had allowed him to sleep; a sleep that was now interrupted by Lambert's noisy arrival back from his recruitment drive in the nearby Mex village. If the noise matched the numbers, Waterman reckoned that the cathouse's yard was occupied by a small army.

He went to the window of the tiny attic-room Babette Dumas had grudgingly given him, to look out on the yard, where at a glance he counted twenty riders, mostly *cantina* dregs, but a few whom he recognized as Americano law-dodgers. Tough, hard-bitten *hombres*, who'd skin a man alive for a dollar.

Waterman shivered.

Babette Dumas had made no secret of the fact that she'd have much preferred if he had fallen off his horse and cracked his skull open, rather than having to assuage the unease his arrival had caused.

On his way upstairs, Waterman had seen the moustachioed face of one man who had hopes of becoming the next territorial governor, from a platform of righteousness. Spence Waterman had made a mental note of his presence in the whorehouse, thinking that in the future, nearer the election in a couple of months time, it was information that he could turn into dollars; *dinero* he might sorely need. The reward he had hoped for from Lambert had not materialized, and he had had strong reservations about riding with him to Skull Pass, doubts that, since he'd woken up, had changed to resolute opposition to any such *loco* adventure.

Strangely, he had got the impression when he had told Lambert about Elinora Langford, that the woman's existence was known to him. And not only known, but that she meant a great deal to him.

Spence Waterman's head filled with the thoughts of facing enraged Indians and a murderous Charles Lambert, if he rumbled his swindler's charade. And waiting in the wings there was Dan Largo, whom he reckoned might prove to be the meanest critter of all.

All considered, another plan began to form in Waterman's devious brain. He hurried out of the attic-room, pausing on the narrow stairs to listen to the sounds of the house. There were still a few grunts, groans and howlings, but in the main the overriding sound was that of snoring. He figured that his plan, simple and direct as it was, should bring in more than sufficient funds to finance his trip to the South Americas. He had heard that down Cuba way a man with resources could greatly embellish them in a short time, with no questions asked. And there was his old pal One-Ear Carter down in Honduras, whom he'd robbed quite a few banks with, and who was still, word had it, robbing banks.

He figured that the men filling the cathouse beds would have come well stacked with dollars to buy their pleasures; cash he planned to relieve them of in place of the uncertain reward from Charles Lambert.

The pompous, Bible-thumping bastard hoping to be the next territorial governor, Spence Waterman reckoned, would be a good starting-point to line his pockets before hitting the trail to Cuba.

16

'Howdy,' Dan Largo greeted the suspicious farmer who held a rifle on him and Elinora Langford. 'I'd be obliged for some grub and filled canteens, mister.'

The farmer remained mute.

'I'm not asking for free sustenance,' Largo said sharply, irked by the farmer's hostility, while also understanding the man's caution. Strangers, within spitting distance of Mexico, would in the main be more dangerous than the rattlers who slithered across the landscape.

The sodbuster relented a little.

'Headed for Mexico?'

'No,' Largo replied.

'Ain't much else to head to in these parts,' said the farmer, whose face held the history of ancestral collusion with the Apache in its features.

Despite his reluctance to elaborate further, Dan Largo knew that if he was not forthcoming the farmer would not give them a mouthful of water. He would probably kill them just as a precaution, like one might kill a wild animal sniffing around, the reasoning being that the animal might be scared off, but might also come back, prepared.

'The lady and me have business on a-ways from here,' Largo informed him.

'Ain't much 'yond here?'

'We're headed to the pass south of here,' Largo volunteered.

'Lots of passes,' the sodbuster probed.

Largo saw Elinora shift uneasily in her saddle. Her unease heightened as Largo elaborated.

'A drunk told us a story about treasure in that pass the Apache regard as sacred.'

'The high one huggin' the Mex border?'

'Yes.'

For a long spell the farmer said

nothing. His eyes switched from Dan Largo to Elinora Langford and back a couple of times before he burst into laughter.

'Something funny?' Largo asked.

Once he controlled his laughter, the farmer said, 'Mister, no one rides into that accursed place and comes back out. And I bin hearin' stories 'bout treasure there since my cradle days.'

He shook his head, as if dealing with the world's greatest fools.

'You take my advice, you'll grub, water-up, and head back to where you've come from.'

Now his expression changed to one of even deeper derision. 'You believed a drunk's story, too, huh?'

His laughter took off again, increasing in robustness until he simply choked for want of breath. He dropped the rifle to his side.

'I ain't got a whole lot in the way o' grub. But I've got a good well, with sweet water.'

They followed him inside the cabin.

'Have you lost your reason, Dan?' Elinora Langford harangued him, as they followed the farmer inside. 'Telling him about Skull Pass.'

'Best he thinks we're *loco*. That's better than him thinking we're dangerous.'

'What if he follows us to the Pass?' she quizzed.

'Why would he want to do that? By his own admission there've been many such as us; treasure-hunters who headed into Skull Pass and were never seen again.' He squeezed Elinora's hand. 'Trust me.'

Seated around the table just a few minutes later, partaking of the meagre meal that the farmer had rustled up, Dan Largo's assurance to Elinora Langford slipped a little on the farmer's curiosity.

'What kinda treasure are you pair supposed to be chasin'?'

Largo chuckled. 'Gold.' His laughter deepened to self-mocking. 'Heck, I've always been a dream-chaser. Ready to latch on to any story of easy pickings.'

His chuckle deepened, and he shook his head. 'I guess we'll take your advice and head back the way we came.'

'Reckon that would be wise, at that,' the farmer opined, quietly.

Largo was uneasy with the man's faraway gaze. He had the look of a man dreaming.

Elinora Langford exchanged a furious look with the gambler. A helpless shrug was all he could come up with by way of reply.

Their hearts skipped a beat when the farmer said, 'A coupla years back there was this dandy kinda fella, south'ner, came through here with a bevvy of slaves in tow. Had this *loco* idea about savin' time by headin' through that pass.'

He shook his head in wonder.

'Wanted to get to Mexico to find a ship to,' he snorted, 'of all places, England.'

The farmer became thoughtful.

'Come to think of it, looked like a

fella who might be totin' a hefty stash, at that.'

'Yeah?' Largo muttered. Shaking his head amusedly, as the farmer had done seconds before. 'If you don't be careful, you'll be dreaming like me.'

An hour later, with the farmer whose name was Ben Fleckton riding along behind them, Elinora Langford intoned scathingly to Largo, 'Trust me!'

'Damn, Elinora,' Largo growled. 'There isn't any such thing as a twist-free trail in these parts. Besides, I reckon an extra gun won't go astray.'

Elinora's tone became even more scathing. 'An extra gun, huh? He can point. That's no proof that he can shoot!'

It was a point well-put and reluctantly accepted by Largo. 'Sometimes a pointed gun is as good as a shooting gun,' he muttered lamely.

As they headed out across the scorched land on the final miles to Skull Pass, Elinora again intoned, 'Trust me. Hah!'

17

While Dan Largo and Elinora Langford, closing on Skull Pass, were pondering on their possible riches, Spence Waterman was dodging from cover to cover on his way to collect his horse from the cathouse livery, or better still, a horse with the kind of stamina that would put fast miles between him and Charles Lambert. Maybe if his luck held, as it had up to now, he'd get on board Lambert's midnight black stallion. That horse, Waterman reckoned, could ride clear to Cuba without breaking his gallop.

He paused, crouched under the kitchen window to check on how far the breakfast had progressed, gauging the kind of time he had to show his heels. He was pleased to see that all the riders who had ridden in with Lambert, including the bossman himself, were partaking of hearty breakfasts which would take a while yet to finish.

He made a dash for the livery. On reaching it, he slid in sideways through the gate. The old-timer who manned the livery was busy feeding and watering the horses being readied for the ride to Skull Pass, and was much too busy grumbling to himself to notice Waterman creeping up on him. As he turned, clutching his slit throat, his eyes were popping in surprise.

Waterman had a way with horses that allowed him to calm the beasts quickly, who were picking up the scent of fresh blood. He hurriedly checked that all was quiet at the house. Then he quickly returned and dragged the old-timer's body into a vacant stall and covered him with hay. He led Lambert's horse from his stall, cooing in the stallion's ear until he had him eating out of his hand. He saddled the horse. On leaving the livery, he resisted the urge to take off at a full gallop. Instead he walked the stallion far enough away, so as not to cause a stir when he gave the horse its head.

His pockets were full of the loot he had robbed from Babette Dumas's guests, all of whom lay with slit throats, occupying beds with equally dead partners. In all, he had collected ten thousand dollars. He spurred the stallion, revelling in the power of the fine beast.

'Cuba, here I come!' he shouted.

He had not counted on a lookout, but he should have. Babette Dumas ran a house where a man's secrets remained between its walls, and fast arriving or fast departing gents were not the norm. Neither did they let out on Firewater — Charles Lambert's magnificent stallion.

The lookout's rifle cracked at the very same second that Lily, a maid in the cathouse, cut loose with a scream that must have woken every sleeper between there and the end of the South Americas.

Spence Waterman felt the waspish

buzz of lead clipping his right earlobe. He ignored the pain and the gush of blood that wet his collar and left shoulder, and wheeled the horse to change direction into a nest of rocks. He found a trail through them, keeping up as much pace as he could, ignoring the danger that could pitch him from the saddle. He hadn't time to take the shooter on. By now his deeds at the cathouse would be known, and Charles Lambert would be seeking his blood.

His devil's luck held; he shucked the lookout. The last he'd seen of that gent was him trying to match Firewater's pace on a broken-down windbag.

Twenty minutes later, the searchers led by a grimfaced Charles Lambert found the lookout impaled on a tree root, where his confused nag had pitched him. Lambert looked to Waterman's dust. He called a one-eyed man over to him, whose name was Blood. Appropriate — he sure had spilled enough of it. He had a reputation as a tracker. He was a lawman turned killer, liking the profits it brought more than his marshal's pay.

Lambert handed Blood his note for a thousand dollars.

'There's a thousand more when you bring me that bastard's head in a bag,' he told the frosty-eyed Blood.

As he rode faster than the wind, with no one in pursuit, Spence Waterman figured that he was clear and free. Lambert would be too preoccupied with getting his hands on Largo and Elinora Langford to be bothered with him, he figured.

The next morning, Spence Waterman spent his final gurgling seconds of life wondering why the tall, frosty-eyed stranger who had just opened his wind-pipe was holding a canvas sack? And why he was switching knives from the stiletto that he had cut his throat with, to the heftier, long-bladed hunting knife.

He had been a fool. He should have known that the best trackers are the ones who leave an empty back-trail, until they are right there beside their quarry.

* * *

An hour passed before Dan Largo left the cover of the rocks he'd taken refuge in on seeing a band of Apaches. It had been a long hour, every second of it filled with worry for Elinora Langford. If the Indians had come upon them, him and Fleckton would have died swiftly. Elinora's death would have been a lot slower and infinitely more degrading and torturous.

The landscape showing no sign of Apaches for the last twenty minutes, Dan Largo decided that it was time to move on. He slid the Peacemaker, which he had had at the ready to shoot Elinora if the Indians had discovered them, back into its holster.

It had been their second unplanned stop. The other unscheduled break in their travels was to allow a cavalry patrol to go by. The army, having their hands full with all sorts of mayhem, discouraged visitors, particularly those close to the Apache sacred place, knowing that any intrusion there would most assuredly stir up a hornets' nest of trouble.

For the next hour their progress was cautious, marked by frequent stops to scan the terrain for any sign of unwelcome predators. He saw no one, but he could feel the burn of watching eyes on him. Finally, he drew rein and looked up at the twisting trail that led up to Skull Pass.

'Anytime now we'll be rich, Dan,' Elinora Langford enthused.

'Or dead,' Largo murmured, as Elinora eagerly took the lead.

18

Heading on up the narrow trail that worryingly provided enough cover to hide a small army, Largo rode on uneasy, an unease that sharpened as they went deeper and deeper into the pass on their journey to its high plateau, the place revered by the Apache. It concerned him that, as the trail became narrower still, neither a quick retreat or a fast forward gallop would be possible.

In fact they were sitting targets, should a shooting war break out.

'You figure there's Apaches 'round?' Ben Fleckton asked Largo in a shaky voice.

'They're here,' the gambler intoned. 'A ghost wouldn't have crossed that open ground for the last couple of miles without being seen. I guess that's why the Indians picked this hellish pass as their sacred place.'

Glancing nervously behind him, above him and all around him, Fleckton said, 'You know, I'm one dumb son-of-a-bitch to be here.'

Dan Largo did not disagree. They were all dumb sons-of-bitches to be there!

'But I figured that this time the story about treasure might just be true,' Fleckton continued.

Largo laughed harshly. 'I guess all the fellas whose bones are bleached in this pass figured that way, Fleckton.' The gambler eyed the farmer. 'You could always turn tail?'

Fleckton, rigid, eyes wide, said, 'Too late!'

Dan Largo followed the farmer's line of vision to the watching Apaches high above them and agreed, 'Yeah. Much too late.'

'There's only five of those red bastards,' Fleckton consoled himself. 'There's three of us. Can the woman shoot?'

'The eye out of a fly,' Largo confirmed.

Ben Fleckton's spirits lifted. 'Guess we ain't in too much of a bind then.'

No sooner had he seen hope than it was dashed by the appearance of another four Indians, farther along the rim of the pass.

'And there's more,' Largo said. 'Probably within spitting distance, too.'

The appearance of the Apaches stalled Elinora Langford's spirited sprint ahead. Her hand reached for her rifle.

'Leave it right where it is!' Largo warned her. In a more kindly tone, he said, 'You pull that Winchester and you'll be wearing wings, Elinora.'

'They've got old carbines. I'd have them wiped out before they could get off a shot, Dan.'

Just then another band of Indians appeared on the opposite rim of the pass.

'How many shots you reckon that rifle's got, Elinora?' the gambler sighed.

'Are we goin' to have to fight our way

outa this?' Fleckton fretted.

'If we keep climbing this trail we will,' Largo said.

'You mean if we turn back now, they'll back off?' Fleckton asked.

'Maybe.'

'I say we do just that,' the farmer said.

'Hell we will!' Elinora Langford grated. 'You go if you want, farmer. Largo and me are going right on up.'

Dan Largo raised an eyebrow, and said pithily, 'Elinora. If we're going to be an item, you'll have to learn to let me make my own decisions, honey.'

Doubt haunted Elinora Langford's green eyes.

'Are you saying you're backing out, Dan?' she asked, in a tone caught between anger and disillusionment.

'All I'm saying, Elinora, is that I make up my own mind,' he replied quietly.

Anger flaring, she said, 'Well, then. Make it up, damn you!'

'I'm going up,' he said, and turning

to Fleckton. 'I reckon you'd be well advised to come along, mister.'

'You said if we backed off now — ' he challenged.

'I said, maybe,' Largo interjected. 'There's no guarantee that you've not already trodden on their ancestors graves.'

He rode on, his words stony. 'The choice is yours farmer.'

A second later, Elinora squealed, 'They're gone!'

This made up Fleckton's mind, and he joined them on the trail upwards. Largo did not bother to tell them that their glee was built on sand. Sure, the Apaches had vanished. The problem was, where had they disappeared to?

19

As a plume of dust rose from the pass trails indicating the Indians' helter-skelter descent — a truly puzzling turn of events — Largo left the trail to see what had got the Indians' urgent attention. Through a pair of egg-shaped rocks leaning against each other for support he saw, far below in the desert, a band of riders also hell-bent on reaching Skull Pass. Dan Largo had no answers to explain this turn of events, but he sure welcomed it.

The fact was that the trio on the trail up to Skull Pass had lost their importance when a scout brought the news of at least twenty riders charging towards the pass. Charles Lambert, by his bullish approach, had done the man he was intent on skinning alive for the murder of his son one great big favour by diverting the attention of the Indians away from the trio. Of course, their problems weren't over by a long shot. It now meant that they had two lots of hide-hunters after them.

But maybe they could reach the pass, find Uncle Willie's diamonds, and make it down the far side to race the short distance to Mexico before the winners of the coming battle regrouped?

It was a wild idea. However, in a lifetime of near-misses, Dan Largo had had his lucky breaks. One more might be all he needed to put him and Elinora on Easy Street.

'What's happening?' Fleckton wondered excitedly.

'Who cares,' Largo said. 'Let's make tracks up this damn mountain to the pass.'

* * *

One of the many flaws in Charles Lambert's character was his tendency to dash in without first planning how he was going to get out, if he had to. But maybe it wasn't a flaw at all; Lambert had gotten used to things going his way during a long line of victories over his adversaries. He was a ruthless man who saw winning as the only outcome of any skirmish he got into, and had few if any qualms about how he won.

Apaches held no terrors for him; he had defeated them many times. However, he failed to understand the commitment and ferocity with which they defended their sacred places — hence his comment in the middle of a battle that was decidedly not going his way.

'What the hell are they getting so het-up about a bone-yard for?'

The man of whom he'd asked the question did not answer. He was much too busy sprinting for his horse to make tracks away from Skull Pass. He never made it. Lambert's bullet smashed into the back of his head, just as he reached his saddle.

As he laid his hired-hand low, an Apache arrow caught Lambert on the shoulder. Gritting his teeth he yanked it free, bringing with the arrowhead a sizeable chunk of flesh, while using his good hand to blast the Indian who was bearing down on him, lance ready to impale him. He dived into the hollow from where he had leapt to shoot the fleeing man, just in time to escape a raft of arrows biting the air above him. His lucky escape meant two other men's misfortune, as the arrows whizzed past to claim them, one receiving an arrow through the windpipe that came out the back of his neck.

Glancing round at his fast-dwindling crew, some of whom had followed the fleeing man's example while Lambert was blasting away at a half-dozen Indians who had laid siege to his cover, he began to wonder if this was the skirmish that would finish him.

He knew that one day there would be such a conflagration, but it galled him to think that he was going to die at the hands of Indians, whom he despised and, like men of his kind, considered them to be inferior to the white man. Nothing more than animals. His one boast had always been that if he had to choose between killing a snake and an Indian, he'd let the snake live. There was no persuading men like Charles Lambert that it was exactly that kind of thinking that had made the settling of the West the bloody carnage that it had been.

When Lambert heard the trumpet, he reckoned that he was on his way to playing a harp, or more likely stoking a fire. He quickly realized that his luck, which had been spectacular all his life, had not run out. He raked the retreating Apaches with gunfire, sending many of them to their Maker as they fled the charging cavalry.

Four of the fleeing Indians charged up the trail leading on up to Skull Pass, clearly bloodthirsty. Lambert reckoned that they were in pursuit of Dan Largo and Elinora Langford, who must already be in the pass, because the Indians had come from there to challenge him, whom they must have seen as the greater threat.

Not bothering to waste time saying thanks to his deliverers, Lambert rounded up the last three men standing of his crew. He took off in furious pursuit after the Apaches, not wanting to give any other man the pleasure of killing Dan Largo, and if needs be, Elinora Langford too — much as he'd regret the waste of having to do so.

* * *

Largo and his partners had made good time to the pass, not that it made any difference that he could see. Frantically, they searched for any sign of the mysterious Vulture's Beak that Uncle Willie had mentioned in his letter to Elinora, that being the place they'd find the cache of diamonds and precious stones.

'What did Uncle Willie mean, Dan?' Elinora wailed in frustration.

Largo had no answers.

Ben Fleckton was bemoaning his misfortune for having partnered a couple of *locos* searching for a damn vulture's beak. Not that there was any shortage of the vile creatures in the skies above the pass, some of them could barely stay aloft, so gorged were they with the feast they had had in the desert below.

Fleckton, convinced that his best course was to try and head down the other side of the mountain while he still had a chance, found no opposition from Dan Largo to the idea. In fact, he reckoned it was a good idea. But Elinora Langford would not abandon her search for the illusive diamonds.

Adamant, she said, 'Uncle Willie was a very meticulous man. If he says there's a vulture's beak around here, Dan, then there damn well is!'

She dropped to the ground exhausted. 'But where, Uncle Willie? Where?'

She told Largo and Fleckton, 'You fellas go if you want. I've waited too long to let go of my dream.'

'Your uncle was a crazy man,' Fleckton said. 'And if he wasn't, then he might have been in one of a hundred other passes hereabouts.'

'Fleckton has a point, Elinora,' Largo said quietly.

'Uncle Willie was right here,' she unequivocally pronounced. Her eyes rolled around the pass. 'I can feel his ghost watching me right now.'

She resumed her frantic search, going over old ground. Suddenly, she dropped to her knees, peering. She began tearing at a mound of recently dislodged rock and shale.

'Over here, Dan.'

Largo joined her. She had already poked a small hole in the mound of debris. At the other side of the opening he could see the mouth of a small cave. Enlisting Fleckton's muscular help, they soon had enough of the rockfall cleared to squeeze through into the cave. Inside was a skeleton. Alongside the skeleton lay a six-gun. Part of the skeleton's skull was blown away, Largo reckoned by the six-gun. On the bony little finger of the right hand was a gold ring, its central diamond embedded in a cluster of smaller diamonds and precious stones. Elinora went and took the ring from the skeleton's finger. The ring sparkled brilliantly, reflecting the fiery glow of the setting sun slanting into the cave.

'Uncle Willie,' Elinora declared.

'I'll take that! It'll do me just fine.'

The cocking of Fleckton's six-gun filled the cave. Largo turned slowly.

'Don't do anything foolish, Fleckton,' he intoned coldly.

'Toss it over here, ma'am,' the farmer ordered. He cautioned Largo. 'Don't do nothin' stupid.' He grabbed the tossed diamond and instructed Elinora, 'You ride with me.'

'I'm not budging from here,' she answered defiantly.

'If you don't, I'll kill him first,' Fleckton promised.

He was nervous enough to do just that, Largo thought.

'I ain't got time to fool around none,' the jittery farmer warned.

Elinora hesitated. Fleckton ranted.

'I'd do as I say. Git over here!'

Largo said, 'Go on, Elinora.' She glanced at him doubtfully. 'Trust me.'

She smiled wryly. 'Wonder where I heard that before?'

Largo waited. His chance came in the second it took for Fleckton to vault into his saddle. He looked away for a fraction of a second, but it was enough time for Dan Largo to act. His Peacemaker left leather in a blur, and sent a bullet into the farmer's chest that lifted him clear of his saddle. The diamond ring flew from his grasp and looped through the air. Elinora strove to grab it and missed. The ring clattered down into a thousand boulders and rocks to be lost forever.

Elinora's pithy swearing was interrupted by the appearance of four howling Apaches, riding hard into the pass. Largo's gun felled the first buck and winged the second. Elinora sprinted for the rifle in her saddle scabbard and was caught in no man's land as the horse reared, excited by the thunder of Largo's Peacemaker and the scent of fresh blood.

One of the bucks, seeing a trophy, swooped on Elinora and grabbed her. As he picked her up, Elinora Langford's razor-sharp reaction to danger, learned in the saloons and Mississippi gambling boats that had been her home since the end of the Civil War, served her well. She clutched the knife from the buck's belt, and drove the blade deep into the Indian's gut.

Meanwhile, Dan Largo had finished off the buck he had winged and was in hand-to-hand combat with the last Apache who had, it seemed to the gambler, the strength of an ox. He drove his knee up into the Indian's groin, but his stranglehold on Largo's throat didn't loosen even a smidgen. He tried to roll the buck. That didn't work either. Soon, nothing would work. He wouldn't have the breath left to even try.

The Indian's blood spattered on Largo's face, as Elinora smashed in his skull with a rock. The buck tried to stand up to meet the new challenge, but Elinora mercilessly whacked him across the face with the bloodied rock, taking most of his face away.

'You know,' Largo croaked. 'You really will have to stop saving my hide, Elinora honey. A man's got his pride, you know.'

She smiled. 'What are partners for, Dan Largo?'

They had little time to bask in their achievement of surviving the Apache onslaught. The arrival of Charles Lambert and his cut-throats, hot on the Apaches' heels, saw to that. Guns cocked and ready, they had Dan Largo and Elinora Langford cold!

20

Addressing Charles Lambert in the way a long time acquaintance might, Elinora Langford said, 'I was wondering when you'd turn up. I was expecting you long before now.'

Lambert's breath was taken away by her statuesque beauty, as it had been that night three years previously on the *Orleans Lady*.

'You two seem very cosy with each other, Elinora?' Largo said, clearly surprised.

'We go back a-ways,' she confirmed.

Lambert had to force himself free of his reverie. He had the business of avenging his son's murder to conclude.

'Did you help murder Rupe, Elinora?' he growled, hoping he could believe her if she said she had not.

He had searched high and low for her after their encounter on the *Orleans*

Lady, and his thirst for her had never really been quenched. She was the first woman whom he could or would treat as an equal; in fact, the kind of woman he'd always searched for. And not having found her, he had opted to take his pleasures with no strings attached at Babette Dumas's cathouse.

'No. And Rupe made all the running to his own grave, Charles,' Elinora told him. 'If you're interested in the truth, I'll tell you what it is. And it's a story that can be backed up by Doc Lonergan back in Spicer's Crossing. Folk say that you respect his word?'

'Lonergan, huh,' he mumbled.

Of the thousands of men he'd met, a lot of whom he'd killed, Horatio Lonergan was the one man who had gained his trust and respect, possessing, as he did, a stubborn streak almost as ornery as his own. He had saved his life too, having been backshot by a hard case employed by an opposing ranch during the fury of range war.

'Are you willing to listen?' Elinora asked.

'Tell your story,' Lambert grunted.

Elinora Langford relayed events from the beginning. From where Rupe Lambert had challenged Dan Largo at the blackjack game, through to Baldwin's treachery at the creek outside of town, to Largo's escape from a hangman's noose on the gambler's arrival back in town.

'He . . . we,' she corrected, 'could have ridden clear, Charles. In fact I thought Largo was *loco* to go back to town. It almost cost him his life.'

Dan Largo stepped in. He unbuckled his gunbelt and dropped it to the ground.

'If you think I killed your son. Then go ahead and shoot, Lambert.'

'I'll oblige.'

Lambert knocked the six-gun from the man's grasp nearest to him. He told Largo, 'You're a gambler, mister. You work the odds. Maybe right now you're taking your biggest gamble, figuring

207

that by throwing down your gun I'll believe your story?'

'If you think that, use that damn gun you've been pointing!' Largo growled.

'You know your son, Charles.' Lambert's eyes switched back to Elinora. 'There was hardly a day went by without him bucking someone, figuring that there was little or no danger in his tomfoolery with you ready to skin alive any man who harmed him.'

She sighed wearily.

'Damn it, Charles. You did Rupe no favours by fighting his fights for him all the time. It just made him think that he could hurt and insult whoever was around when his humour soured.'

Emphatically, she stated: 'Rupe was weak, Charles. And without you saving his neck more times than you can count, he'd have long since been killed.'

She finished wearily. 'It was a miracle he lived so long. And you know it.'

Lambert strangled on the words he was trying to get out.

'Ah, shush!' Elinora Langford

scolded him. 'You know the truth of what I've said!'

Lambert slumped in the saddle, seeming inches shorter than he had been, and as deflated as a windless concertina. Years piled on him, and he was suddenly an old man. He admitted, 'I tried to make Rupe into the kind of man I wanted him to be, Elinora. But he wasn't the stuff of manhood.'

Unsympathetically, Elinora said, 'Rupe would have been a man in his own way and in his own right, if you hadn't dogged him all the way, trying to mould him in your image. You had your life. You should have let Rupe have his, Charles.'

'If you want,' Largo offered Lambert, 'we'll ride back to Spicer's Crossing with you. Let Doc Lonergan tell his story.'

'No need,' Lambert replied listlessly.

The setting sun flashed over the pointed peaks of Skull Pass, filling the pass with eerie shadows from which Largo had no doubt ghosts watched.

Broken in spirit, Charles Lambert wheeled his horse about, and began back down the trail.

Dan Largo and Elinora Langford watched him out of sight.

'I reckon we'd best ride too, Dan,' Elinora said.

'What about Uncle Willie's cache of diamonds?'

'Oh, the diamonds don't seem to matter any more. Anyway, we could spend our lives poking around in this accursed place, and be as close to finding the diamonds then as we are now.'

She placed her head on Largo's shoulder. The setting sun sparkled in her red hair.

'Besides,' she murmured. 'I've got other plans, Dan Largo.'

She raised her mouth to his. Their kiss was long and passionate, until suddenly Largo pulled away with an exclamation.

'I'll be damned!

'Not if you keep jumping away you

won't,' Elinora complained, piqued as any woman would be by what appeared to be Largo's disinterest in a heated clinch.

He grabbed her and swung her around. 'Look, Elinora. Look, gal!'

The slanting sun on the ragged peaks of the pass was creating a shadow that held them breathlessly mesmerized.

'The sunset,' Elinora said excitedly. 'In his letter, Uncle Willie mentioned the sunset.'

As the sun dipped below the peaks, the shadow of the vulture's beak grew in length, until it poked into a niche in the rock face.

Elinora ran to the place. Largo pulled her back.

'Careful,' he cautioned. 'You never know what kind of critter might be lurking in there.'

He snapped off the branch of a dead tree and used it to poke around inside the niche on the rock face. Satisfied that there was no nasty surprises in store, he reached his hand in and withdrew a velvet pouch with faded gold lettering that spelled GREENGLADES.

He handed the bag to Elinora.

Breathlessly, she opened the pouch and spilled its glittering contents into Largo's cupped hands. The treasure-trove of diamonds and precious stones filled his cupped hands to overflowing.

'There's a fortune here,' he murmured in awe.

A sudden shaft of dying sunlight flashed between the peaks of the pass to set the treasure in Dan Largo's hands on fire, and then vanished as quickly as it had appeared to let darkness in.

'Thank you Uncle Willie,' Elinora murmured. 'You did well.'

A sudden breeze swirled through the pass.

After a long time, Elinora asked, 'London or Paris first, Dan?'

Largo shifted uneasily.

'What is it?'

'Well, there's this big poker game in Dodge that I've always wanted to sit in on,' he said. 'But never had the poke to buy in.'

'Dodge?' Elinora groaned.

'Trust me, Elinora honey,' he pleaded.

She smiled. 'Then, London and Paris?'

'Nope.'

'No?'

'Nope.' Laughing he drew her into his arms. 'Then we find a preacher. After all, a man can't take the woman he loves to London and Paris, France, without seeing to the proper formalities first! And after . . . '

'After?' Elinora asked quietly.

He picked up the worn velvet bag that had held the diamonds and precious stones. His finger traced the faded gold letters.

'After,' he said. 'We're going to rebuild Greenglades.'

With a contented sigh, Elinora Langford sank into Dan Largo's arms.

We do hope that you have enjoyed reading this large print book.

Did you know that all of our titles are available for purchase?

We publish a wide range of high quality large print books including:
**Romances, Mysteries, Classics
General Fiction
Non Fiction and Westerns**

Special interest titles available in large print are:
**The Little Oxford Dictionary
Music Book, Song Book
Hymn Book, Service Book**

Also available from us courtesy of Oxford University Press:
**Young Readers' Dictionary
(large print edition)
Young Readers' Thesaurus
(large print edition)**

For further information or a free brochure, please contact us at:
**Ulverscroft Large Print Books Ltd.,
The Green, Bradgate Road, Anstey,
Leicester, LE7 7FU, England.
Tel:** (00 44) **0116 236 4325**
Fax: (00 44) **0116 234 0205**

Other titles in the
Linford Western Library:

A TOWN CALLED TROUBLESOME

John Dyson

Matt Matthews had carved his ranch out of the wild Wyoming frontier. But he had his troubles. The big blow of '86 was catastrophic, with dead beeves littering the plains, and the oncoming winter presaged worse. On top of this, a gang of desperadoes had moved into the Snake River valley, killing, raping and rustling. All Matt can do is to take on the killers single-handed. But will he escape the hail of lead?

THE WIND WAGON

Troy Howard

Sheriff Al Corning was as tough as they came and with his four seasoned deputies he kept the peace in Laramie — at least until the squatters came. To fend off starvation, the settlers took some cattle off the cowmen, including Jonas Lefler. A hard, unforgiving man, Lefler retaliated with lynchings. Things got worse when one of the squatters revealed he was a former Texas lawman — and no mean shooter. Could Sheriff Corning prevent further bloodshed?